REDHEAD BY THE
SIDE OF THE ROAD

Anne Tyler was born in Minneapolis, Minnesota, in 1941 and grew up in Raleigh, North Carolina. Her bestselling novels include *Breathing Lessons, The Accidental Tourist, Dinner at the Homesick Restaurant, Ladder of Years, Back When We Were Grownups, A Patchwork Planet, The Amateur Marriage, Digging to America, A Spool of Blue Thread, Vinegar Girl* and *Clock Dance*.

In 1989 she won the Pulitzer Prize for *Breathing Lessons*; in 1994 she was nominated by Roddy Doyle and Nick Hornby as 'the greatest novelist writing in English'; in 2012 she received the Sunday Times Award for Literary Excellence; and in 2015 *A Spool of Blue Thread* was a *Sunday Times* bestseller and was shortlisted for the Baileys Women's Prize for Fiction and the Man Booker Prize.

Redhead by the Side of the Road

ANNE TYLER

Chatto & Windus

LONDON

1 3 5 7 9 10 8 6 4 2

Chatto & Windus, an imprint of Vintage,
20 Vauxhall Bridge Road,
London SW1V 2SA

Chatto & Windus is part of the Penguin Random House group of companies
whose addresses can be found at global.penguinrandomhouse.com

Penguin
Random House
UK

First published in the United Kingdom by Chatto & Windus in 2020
First published in the United States by Alfred A. Knopf in 2020

penguin.co.uk/vintage

A CIP catalogue record for this book is available from the British Library

HB ISBN 9781784743475
TPB ISBN 9781784743482

Printed and bound in Great Britain by Clays Ltd, Elcograf S.p.A.

Penguin Random House is committed to a sustainable future
for our business, our readers and our planet. This book is made
from Forest Stewardship Council® certified paper.

Redhead
by the
Side of
the Road

I

YOU HAVE TO WONDER what goes through the mind of a man like Micah Mortimer. He lives alone; he keeps to himself; his routine is etched in stone. At seven fifteen every morning you see him set out on his run. Along about ten or ten thirty he slaps the magnetic TECH HERMIT sign onto the roof of his Kia. The times he leaves on his calls will vary, but not a day seems to go by without several clients requiring his services. Afternoons he can be spotted working around the apartment building; he moonlights as the super. He'll be sweeping the walk or shaking out the mat or conferring with a plumber. Monday nights, before trash day, he hauls the garbage bins to the alley; Wednesday nights, the recycling bins. At ten p.m. or so the three squinty windows behind the foundation plantings go dark. (His apartment is in the basement. It is probably not very cheery.)

He's a tall, bony man in his early forties with not-so-good posture—head lunging slightly forward, shoulders slightly hunched. Jet-black hair, but when he neglects to shave for a day his whiskers have started coming in gray. Blue eyes, heavy eyebrows, hollows in his cheeks. A clamped-looking mouth. Unvarying outfit of jeans and a T-shirt or a sweatshirt, depending on the season, with a partially-erased-looking brown leather jacket when it's really cold. Scuffed brown round-toed shoes that seem humble, like a schoolboy's shoes. Even his running shoes are plain old dirty-white sneakers—none of the fluorescent stripes and gel-filled soles and such that most runners favor—and his shorts are knee-length denim cutoffs.

He has a girlfriend, but they seem to lead fairly separate lives. You see her heading toward his back door now and then with a sack of takeout; you see them setting forth on a weekend morning in the Kia, minus the TECH HERMIT sign. He doesn't appear to have male friends. He is cordial to the tenants but no more than that. They call out a greeting when they meet up with him and he nods amiably and raises a hand, often not troubling to speak. Nobody knows if he has family.

The apartment building's in Govans—a small, three-story brick cube east of York Road in north Baltimore, with a lake-trout joint on the right and a used-clothing store on the left. Tiny parking lot out back. Tiny plot of grass in front. An incongruous front porch—just a concrete slab stoop, really—with a splintery wooden porch swing that nobody ever sits in, and a vertical row of doorbells next to the dingy white door.

Does he ever stop to consider his life? The meaning of it, the point? Does it trouble him to think that he will probably spend his next thirty or forty years this way? Nobody knows. And it's almost certain nobody's ever asked him.

On a Monday toward the end of October, he was still eating breakfast when his first call came in. Usually his morning went: a run, a shower, then breakfast, and then a little tidying up. He hated it when something interrupted the normal progression. He pulled his phone from his pocket and checked the screen: EMILY PRESCOTT. An old lady; he had dealt with her often enough that her name was in his directory. Old ladies had the easiest problems to fix but the greatest number of fractious questions. They always wanted to know *why*. "How come this happened?" they would ask. "Last night when I went to bed my computer was just fine and this morning it's all kerblooey. But I didn't do a thing to it! I was sound asleep!"

"Yeah, well, never mind, now I've got it fixed," he would say.

"But why did it *need* fixing? What made it go wrong?"

"That's not the kind of question you want to ask about a computer."

"Why not?"

On the other hand, old ladies were his bread and butter, plus this one lived nearby in Homeland. He pressed Talk and said, "Tech Hermit."

"Mr. Mortimer?"

"Yo."

"It's Emily Prescott; remember me? I have a dire emergency."

"What's up?"

"Why, I can't seem to get my computer to go anywhere at all! It just completely refuses! Won't go to any websites! And yet I still have a Wi-Fi signal!"

"Did you try rebooting?" he asked.

"What's that?"

"Turning it off and then on again, like I showed you?"

"*Oh*, yes. 'Sending it for a time-out,' I like to call that." She gave a flutter of a laugh. "I did try, yes. It didn't help."

"Okay," he said. "How's about I come by around eleven."

"Eleven o'clock?"

"Right."

"But I wanted to get a present for my granddaughter's birthday on Wednesday, and I need to order it early enough for the free two-day delivery."

He stayed quiet.

"Well," she said. She sighed. "All right: eleven. I'll be waiting. You remember the address?"

"I remember."

He hung up and took another bite of toast.

His place was bigger than you might expect, given that it was in the basement. A single long, open space for the living room and the kitchen combined, and then two small, separate bedrooms and a bathroom. The ceiling was a decent height, and the floor was paved with not-too-shabby composition tiles in a streaky ivory color. A beige scatter rug lay in front of the couch. The minimal windows up close to the ceiling didn't allow much of a view, but he could always tell if the sun was shining—which it was, today—and now that the trees had started to turn he could see a few dry leaves collecting around the roots of the azalea bushes. Later he might take a rake to those.

He finished the last of his coffee and then pushed back his chair and stood up and carried his dishes to the sink. He had a system: he set the dishes to soak while he wiped the table and countertop, put away the butter, ran his stick vacuum under his chair in case he'd dropped any crumbs. His actual vacuuming day was Friday, but he liked to keep on top of things betweentimes.

Monday was floor-mopping day—the kitchen floor and the bathroom. "Zee dreaded moppink," he said as he ran hot water into a bucket. He often talked to himself as he worked, using one or another foreign accent. Right now it was German, or maybe Russian. "Zee moppink of zee floors." He didn't bother vacuuming the bathroom first, because there was no need; the floor was still pristine from last week. It was Micah's personal theory that if you actually noticed the difference you made when you cleaned—the coffee table suddenly shiny, the rug suddenly lint-free—it meant you had waited too long to do it.

Micah prided himself on his housekeeping.

When he'd finished mopping he emptied his bucket down the sink in the laundry room. He propped his mop against the water heater. Then he went back into the apartment and tackled the living area, folding the afghan on the couch and tossing out a couple of beer cans and slapping the cushions into shape. His furnishings were sparse—just the couch and the coffee table and an ugly brown vinyl recliner chair. Everything had been here when he moved in; all he'd added was a metal utility shelf for his tech magazines and his manuals. Any other reading he did—mostly mysteries and biographies—he got from the free-book place and gave back when he had finished. Otherwise he'd have had to buy more shelving.

By now the kitchen floor had dried, and he returned to wash the breakfast dishes and wipe them and put them away. (Some might leave them to air-dry, but Micah hated the cluttered appearance of dishes sitting out in a draining rack.) Then he put on his glasses—rimless distance glasses for driving—and grabbed the car topper and his carryall and left through the back door.

His back door was at the rear of the building, at the bottom of a flight of concrete steps that led up to the parking lot. He paused after he'd climbed the steps to assess the weather: warmer now than when he had taken his run, and the breeze had died. He'd been right not to bother with his jacket. He clamped the TECH HERMIT sign onto his car and then slid in, started the engine, and raised a hand to Ed Allen, who was plodding toward his pickup with his lunchbox.

When Micah was behind the wheel he liked to pretend he was being evaluated by an all-seeing surveillance system. Traffic God, he called it. Traffic God was operated by a fleet of men in shirtsleeves and green visors who frequently commented to one another on the perfection of Micah's driving. "Notice how he uses his turn signal even when no one's behind him," they would say. Micah always, always used his turn signal. He used it in his own parking lot, even. Accelerating, he dutifully pictured an egg beneath his gas pedal; braking, he glided to an almost undetectable stop. And whenever some other driver decided at the last minute that he needed to switch to Micah's lane, you could count on Micah to slow down and turn his left palm upward in a courtly after-you gesture. "See that?" the guys at Traffic God would say to one another. "Fellow's manners are impeccable."

It eased the tedium some, at least.

He turned onto Tenleydale Road and parked alongside the curb. But just as he was reaching for his carryall, his cell phone rang. He pulled it from his pocket and raised his glasses to his forehead so he could check the screen. CASSIA SLADE. That was unusual. Cass was his woman friend (he refused to call anyone in her late thirties a "girlfriend"), but they didn't usually speak at this hour. She should be at work now, knee-deep in fourth-graders. He punched Talk. "What's up?" he asked.

"I'm going to be evicted."

"What?"

"Evicted from my apartment." She had a low, steady voice that Micah approved of, but right now there was a telltale tightness to it.

"How can you be evicted?" he asked her. "It isn't even your place."

"No, but Nan came by this morning without telling me ahead," she said. Nan was the actual renter. She lived now with her fiancé in a condo down near the harbor, but she had never given up her claim on the apartment, which Micah could understand even if Cass could not. (You don't want to seal off all your exits.) "She just rang the doorbell, no warning," Cass said, "so I didn't have time to hide the cat."

"Oh. The cat," Micah said.

"I was hoping he wouldn't show himself. I was blocking her view as best I could and hoping she wouldn't want to come inside, but she said, 'I just need to pick up my— what is *that*?' and she was staring past me at Whiskers who was peeking out from the kitchen doorway big as life when ordinarily, *you* know Whiskers; he can't abide a stranger. I tried to tell her I hadn't *planned* on having a cat. I explained how I'd just found him in the window well out front. But Nan said, 'You're missing the point; you know I'm deathly allergic. One whiff of a room where a cat's merely passed through a month ago,' she said, 'one little *hair* of a cat, left behind on a rug, and I just—oh, Lord, I can already feel my throat closing up!' And then she backed out onto the landing and waved me off when I tried to follow. 'Wait!' I said, but 'I'll be in touch,' she told me, and you know what *that* means."

"No, I don't know any such thing," Micah said. "So, she'll call you up tonight and ream you out and you will apologize and that's that. Except you'll have to get rid of Whiskers, I guess."

"I can't get rid of Whiskers! He's just finally feeling at home here."

Micah thought of Cass as basically a no-nonsense woman, so this cat business always baffled him. "Look," he told her. "You're way ahead of yourself. All she's said so far is she will be in touch."

"And where would I move to?" Cass asked.

"Nobody's said a word about moving."

"Not *yet*," she told him.

"Well, wait till she does before you start packing, hear?"

"And it's not so easy to find a place that allows pets," Cass said, as if he hadn't spoken. "What if I end up homeless?"

11

"Cass. There are *hundreds* of people with pets, living all over Baltimore. You'll find another place, trust me."

There was a silence. He could make out the voices of children at the other end of the line, but they had a faraway sound. She must be out on the playground; it must be recess time.

"Cass?"

"Well, thanks for listening," she said abruptly. She clicked off.

He stared at the screen a moment before he slid his glasses back down and tucked his phone away.

"Am I the very dumbest old biddy among all your clients?" Mrs. Prescott asked him.

"No, not at all," he told her truthfully. "You're not even in the top ten."

Her wording amused him, because she did look a little bit henlike. She had a small, round head and a single pillowy mound of breasts-plus-belly atop her toothpick legs. Even here at home she wore little heels that gave her walk a certain jerky quality.

Micah was sitting on the floor beneath her desk, which was a massive antique rolltop with surprisingly limited work space. (People put their computers in the most outlandish locations. It was as if they didn't quite grasp that they weren't still writing with fountain pens.) He had unplugged two of the cords from the tangle attached to the surge protector—one cord labeled MODEM and the other labeled ROUTER, both in his own firm uppercase—and he was gazing at the second hand on his wristwatch. "Okay," he said finally. He reattached the modem cord and went back to studying his second hand.

"My friend Glynda? You don't know her," Mrs. Prescott said, "but I keep telling her she ought to get in touch with you. She is *scared* of her computer! She only uses it to email. She doesn't want to give it any *information*, she says. I told her about your little book."

"Mm-hmm," Micah said. His book was called *First, Plug It In*. It was one of Woolcott Publishing's better-selling titles, but Woolcott was strictly local and he didn't have a hope the book would ever make him rich.

He reattached the router cord and began extricating himself from underneath the desk. "This here is the hardest part of my job," he told Mrs. Prescott as he struggled to his knees. He grabbed on to the desk frame and rose to a standing position.

"Oh, pshaw, you're too young to talk that way," Mrs. Prescott said.

"Young! I'll be forty-four on my next birthday."

"Exactly," Mrs. Prescott said. And then, "I did tell Glynda you sometimes give lessons, but she claimed she would forget it all two minutes after you left."

"She's right," Micah said. "She ought to just buy my book."

"But lessons are so much more—oh! Look at that!"

She was staring at her computer screen, both hands clasped beneath her chin. "Amazon!" she said in a thrilled tone.

"Yep. Now. Were you watching what I did?"

"Well, I . . . Not exactly, no."

"I turned off your computer; I unplugged the modem cord; I unplugged the router cord. See there where they're labeled?"

"Oh, Mr. Mortimer, I would never remember all that!"

"Suit yourself," he said. He reached for his clipboard on the top of her desk and started making out her bill.

"I'm thinking of ordering my granddaughter an African-American baby doll," Mrs. Prescott said. "What do you think of that?"

"Is your granddaughter African-American?"

"Why, no."

"Then I think it would just look weird," he said.

"Oh, Mr. Mortimer! I certainly hope not!"

He tore off the top copy of her bill and handed it to her. "I feel bad even charging you," he told her, "what with the piddly amount of work I did."

"Now, don't you talk that way," she said. "You saved my life! I ought to pay you triple." And she went off to fetch her checkbook.

The fact was, he reflected as he was driving home, that even if she *had* paid him triple, this job barely supported him. On the other hand, it was work he liked, and at least he was his own boss. He wasn't all that fond of people ordering him around.

Once upon a time, more had been expected of him. He'd been the first in his family to go to college; his father had pruned trees for Baltimore Gas and Electric and his mother had waited tables, as did all four of his sisters to this day. They'd viewed Micah as their shining star. Until he wasn't anymore. For one thing, he'd had to take a number of odd jobs to flesh out his partial scholarship, which had made keeping up with his studies kind of a struggle. More important, though: college just wasn't how he'd pictured it. He had thought it would be a place that would give him all the answers, that would provide a single succinct Theory of Everything to organize his world by, but instead it seemed an extension of high school: same teachers at the front of the room repeating things over and over, same students yawning and fidgeting and whispering among themselves throughout the lectures. He lost his enthusiasm. He floundered about; he changed majors twice; he ended up in computer science, which was at least something definite— something yes-or-no, black-or-white, as logical and orderly as a game of dominoes. Midway through his senior year (which had taken him five years to get to), he dropped out to start a software company with a classmate named Deuce Baldwin. Deuce provided the money and Micah provided the brainpower—specifically, a program of his own invention that sorted and archived emails. Now it would be a dinosaur, of course. The world had moved on. But at the time it had filled a real need, which made it even more unfortunate when Deuce had proved impossible to get along with. Rich guys! They were all the same. Forever throwing their weight around, acting so entitled. Things had gone from bad to worse, till cut to the chase and Micah walked out. He couldn't even take his program with him, because he hadn't had the foresight to nail down his rights to it.

He turned into his space on the lot and cut the engine. His watch read 11:47. "Flawless," Traffic God murmured. Micah had made the whole trip without a single misstep, a single fumble or correction.

Really, his life was good. He had no reason to feel unhappy.

A man needed the viruses stripped off his computer, and a mom-and-pop grocery store wanted to start billing its customers online. In between, Micah checked out a faulty wall switch in 1B. 1B was Yolanda Palma, a dramatic-looking woman in maybe her early fifties with a flaring mane of dark hair and a mournful, sagging face. "So what's new in *your* life?" she asked as she watched him test the voltage. She always behaved as if they were old friends, which they weren't. "Oh," he said, "not much," but he might as well not have spoken, because she was already saying, "Me, I'm at it again. Joined a whole new dating service and started over. Some folks never learn, I guess."

"How's that working out?" he asked. The wall switch was dead as a doornail.

"Well, last night I met this guy for a drink at Swallow at the Hollow. A real-estate inspector. He claimed he was six foot one, but you know how *that* goes. And he could've stood to lose a few pounds, although who am I to talk, right? Anyhow, turns out that he'd been divorced for three and a half weeks. Three and a *half*, like he'd been counting the days, and not in a good way. Like his divorce had been a personal tragedy. And sure enough, straight off he has to tell how his ex-wife was so gorgeous she could have been a model. How she wore a size two dress. How she didn't own a single pair of shoes that weren't stilettos and therefore the tendons in her heels or something had shortened so her toes were permanently pointed. If she walked barefoot to the bathroom at night she had to walk tippy-toe. He made it sound like that was an attractive quality, but all I could picture was a woman with sort of *hooves*, know what I mean?"

"I'm going to have to pick up a new switch before I can fix this," Micah told her.

She was lighting a cigarette now and had to exhale before she spoke. "Okay," she said offhandedly, dropping her lighter back into her pocket. "So we have one drink and then I say I'd better be getting home. 'Home!' he says. Says, 'I was thinking we might go to my place.' And he reaches over and clamps a hand on my knee and gazes meaningfully into my eyes. I look back at him. I freeze. I don't say a word. Finally he takes his hand away and says, 'Well, or else not, I guess.'"

"Ha," Micah said.

He was replacing the switch plate now. Yolanda watched thoughtfully, batting her smoke away with one hand each time she exhaled. "Tonight it's a dentist," she said.

"You're trying *again*?"

"This one's never been married. I don't know if that's a good thing or a bad thing."

Micah bent to put his screwdriver back in his tool bucket. "Might be another day or two before I get to the hardware store," he told her.

"I'm around," she said.

She was always around, it seemed to him. He didn't know what she did for a living.

As she was seeing him out, she asked, "What do you think?" and flashed him a sudden fierce grimace, showing all her teeth which were large and extremely straight-edged, like a double row of piano keys.

He said, "About what?"

"Would a dentist approve, do you think?"

"Sure," he said.

Although he suspected a dentist might have something to say about her smoking.

"He sounded really nice when he texted me," she said.

And all at once she brightened, so that her features no longer looked saggy.

On Monday evenings, he and Cass didn't usually get together. But his last call of the day came from a podiatry office out past the Beltway, and as he was driving home afterward he happened to notice the scribbly red-and-white sign on his left for his favorite barbecue place. On impulse, he turned into the parking lot and sent a text to Cass. *How about I bring some Andy Nelson over for supper?* he asked. She answered right away, which meant she must be home from work already. *Good idea!* she said. So he cut the engine and went in to place an order.

By then it was after five, and he had to wait in a milling crowd of workmen in baggy coveralls, and young couples draped all over each other, and harried-looking women ringed by clamoring children. The smells of smoke and vinegar made him hungry; all he'd had for lunch was a peanut-butter-and-raisin sandwich. He ended up ordering about twice as much as he should have: not only ribs but collard greens and potato wedges and cornbread besides, enough to fill two plastic bags. Then for his entire trip down the expressway he was tormented by the smells drifting from the backseat.

Rush hour was in full swing and the car radio warned of

delays, but Micah disengaged his mind and let his hands rest loosely on the wheel. The hills in the distance seemed to be oxidizing, he noticed. Overnight, the trees had turned a hazy orange color.

Cass lived off Harford Road in what could be mistaken for a one-family house, graying white clapboard with a small front porch, but just inside the foyer a flight of stairs on the right led to her second-floor apartment. At the top of the stairs Micah shifted one of his bags in order to knock on the door. "That smells heavenly," Cass said when she let him in. She took a bag from him and turned to lead the way to the kitchen.

"I was out in Cockeysville and my car just sort of veered into the parking lot," he told her. "I think I might have ordered too much, though." He set his bag on the counter and gave her a quick kiss.

She was still in her teacher outfit—skirt of some kind, sweater of some kind, something muted and unexceptional which he approved of without really noticing. He approved of her appearance in general, really. She was a tall, slow-moving woman with substantial breasts and wide hips, sturdy calves rising from her matronly black pumps. In fact she was matronly altogether, which Micah found kind of a turn-on. He seemed to have outgrown any interest in the slip-of-a-girl type. Her face was broad and calm, and her eyes were a deep gray-green, and her wheat-colored hair hung straight almost to her shoulders, casually parted and indifferently styled. He considered her restful to look at.

She had already set the kitchen table and placed a roll of paper towels at the center, because mere napkins were inadequate when you were eating barbecued ribs. While she was opening the bags and putting out the food, Micah took two cans of beer from the fridge. He gave one to her and sat down across from her with the other.

"How was your day?" she asked him.

"It was okay. How was yours?"

"Well, other than Nan finding out about Whiskers . . ."

"Oh. Right," he said. He'd forgotten.

"When I got home from work she'd left a message on my phone asking me to call her."

Micah waited. Cass served herself some collard greens and passed him the container.

"So what did she have to say?" he asked finally.

"I don't know yet."

"You didn't call?"

Cass selected three ribs from their Styrofoam box, firming her lips in a way that struck Micah as obstinate. He had a sudden inkling as to what she might have looked like as a child.

"There's no sense putting it off," he told her. "You're only prolonging things."

"I'll get to it," she said shortly.

He decided not to pursue the subject. He chomped down on a rib.

Every waking moment that Cass spent in her apartment, she seemed to have some sort of music or news or *something* filling the airwaves. In the mornings it was NPR; in the evenings the TV was on whether or not she was watching: and during meals an endless stream of easy-listening tunes flowed mellifluously from the kitchen radio. Micah, who appreciated silence, would shut all this out for a while but then gradually grow aware of a vague sense of unfocused irritability, and that was when he would notice what he was hearing. Now he said, "Could we turn that down a notch?" Cass sent him a resigned look and reached over to lower the volume. He would have preferred for her to shut it off completely, but he supposed that was asking too much.

He and Cass had been together for three years or so, and they had reached the stage where things had more or less solidified: compromises arrived at, incompatibilities adjusted to, minor quirks overlooked. They had it down to a system, you could say.

Not till they were halfway through the meal did Cass return to the subject of Nan. "I mean, look at what *she's* got," she said. Micah wasn't sure at first what she was talking about, but then she said, "An enormous golden retriever! Well, okay, it's her fiancé's dog, but still. You would think she could understand why I can't get rid of Whiskers."

It had always struck Micah as unlike Cass to give her cat such a cutesy name. Why not something more dignified? Why not Herman? Or George? But of course he never mentioned this. "Where *is* Whiskers?" he thought to ask now. He glanced around the kitchen, but there was no sign of him.

"That's the irony," Cass said. "You know how he disappears whenever I have company. It's only by pure blind chance that he happened to poke his nose out while Nan was at the door."

"Well, more to the point," he said, "when is Nan going to give this place up and let you take over the lease? She's been engaged to that guy for longer than I've known you."

"Good question," Cass said. "Other people meet, they fall in love, they move in together, they marry. But Nan didn't get the memo, it seems."

Micah let a brief pause develop and then he asked what Deemolay had been up to—her most troubled, most disruptive student. Deemolay caused chaos the instant he entered the classroom, but he lived in a car with his grandmother and Micah knew Cass had a soft spot in her heart for him.

Deemolay had poked a plastic ruler into Jennaya's back at lunchtime and told her it was a switchblade. *That* was an interesting topic.

After supper they cleared the table, stacking the dishes on the counter because Cass didn't share Micah's belief that they should clean up before they left the kitchen. Cass's dishes were actual china, and her cutlery came in a set, and she owned numerous nonessentials like a lettuce dryer and a knife rack. Not only that, but the furniture in her living room was substantial and deeply cushioned, and all her linens matched each other, and houseplants and ceramic doodads dotted her many small tables. Micah found this a bit claustrophobic, but at the same time he was impressed. He sometimes felt that his own place didn't look quite grown-up.

They relocated to the living room to watch the evening news, sitting together on the couch on either side of the cat, who had finally deigned to make an appearance. He was a skinny black adolescent with, yes, noticeably long white whiskers, and he hunched between them purring with his eyes closed. The TV had to compete with the music still playing from the kitchen, until Micah finally rose and went to switch off the radio. He didn't know how Cass endured that constant flow of sound. It made his brain feel fractured.

If it were up to him, he would have done without the news as well. Micah had about given up on this country, to tell the truth. It seemed to be going to hell these days, and he didn't have the sense he could do anything about it. But Cass was very conscientious, and she insisted on absorbing every depressing detail. She sat erect in the darkened living room and watched intently, the light from the TV gilding her profile and the curve of her throat. Micah loved the curve of her throat. He leaned closer and set his lips to the pulse just below her jaw, and she tilted her head to rest it on his, briefly, but kept her eyes on the screen. "Every day's worth of harm we do the planet will take a decade to reverse," she told him. "And some of it we can *never* reverse."

"Why don't I spend the night tonight," Micah murmured in her ear.

"You know tomorrow's a school day," she said, patting his hand.

"Just this once," he told her, "and I promise I'll wake up early and clear out of here."

But she said, "Micah?"

Her questioning tone implied that he was being unreasonable; he had no idea why. Almost always she agreed to let him stay. But she drew away from him and said, "Besides, I thought this was your night to set the garbage bins out."

"I can do it first thing in the morning," he said.

"And I haven't finished my grading!" she told him.

He knew when he was defeated. He sighed and said, "Okay, okay." And when the next commercial came on, he rose to leave.

"Don't you want your leftovers?" she asked as she followed him to the door.

He said, "You can keep them."

"Well, thank you."

"Hey!" he said. He turned to face her. "Maybe tomorrow

I could fix my world-famous chili. And you could come for supper and bring the rest of the cornbread."

"Oh, I don't know . . ."

"Chili on top of cornbread! Yum!" he said enticingly.

"Well," she said, "I guess. If we make it early." And she opened the door and gave him a real kiss, finally, and stood back to let him go.

Driving home, he had the streets almost to himself, but he stayed under the speed limit anyway. He didn't hold with the theory that the law allowed a tad bit of wiggle room. If thirty-five miles per hour really meant thirty-eight, they ought to go ahead and *say* thirty-eight.

"The man talks sense," Traffic God commented approvingly.

Micah headed west on Northern Parkway. He turned left on York—signaling first, of course, even though he was in the left-turn-only lane. At the back of his mind, he felt a prickly little burr of unease. It seemed to him that Cass had acted less affectionate than usual. Since when had she cared if it was his night to set the garbage bins out? But she wasn't the type to go into those mysterious sulks the way some women did, so he shook the feeling off. He started whistling "Moonlight in Vermont," which was the last tune her kitchen radio had been playing.

Farther down York Road the little stores and cafés grew more familiar. Most of the stores were closed by now, their neon signs unlighted and barely visible in the dusk. He took a left onto Roscoe Street and then a right just before the used-clothing store, heading toward the parking lot.

When he got out of the car he retrieved his carryall from the passenger seat and plucked his TECH HERMIT sign off the roof and set them both at the top of his steps. Then he started wheeling the garbage bins to the alley. 2B's bin—Mr. Lane's—had a long cardboard mailing tube slanting out from under the lid. Recycling, on a garbage day! "Ooh-la-la, monsieur," he said reproachfully. "You are un pee-*saw*," which was how he thought the French might pronounce "pissant." And he shook his head as he parked the bin next to 2A's.

Some people; they just didn't have a clue.

2

EARLY THE FOLLOWING MORNING, when he was
just approaching the edge of waking up, Micah
dreamed he found a baby in a supermarket aisle. He
rounded a corner and there it was, sitting erect on the floor
in front of the breakfast cereals and wearing nothing but a
diaper.

He stopped short and stared at it. The baby stared back,
cheerfully—a round-faced, pink-cheeked, generic sort of
baby with a skimming of short blond hair. There wasn't a
sign of another grown-up around.

Micah rose to consciousness slowly, as if his sleep had lay-
ers to it. He opened his eyes and blinked at the ceiling. He
was still trying to figure out what to do about the baby. Take
it to Lost and Found, he supposed, but this meant picking it
up, and he worried it would start crying. Then its parents
would rush to the rescue, and they might very possibly leap
to the wrong conclusion—accuse him of kidnapping, even.

How to convince them he'd meant no harm? He knew it didn't look good.

He turned off his alarm before the radio could click on and he struggled out of bed, but the baby stayed in his mind. He couldn't understand why it had seemed so unperturbed. So expectant, even, as if it had been certain that Micah would show up. And once he was out on his run, taking gulps of the nippy air, he had the incongruous thought that he would startle the baby to bits right now if he were to wrap his cold hands around its naked torso.

He grimaced and picked up speed, shaking off the dream's last traces.

At this hour, he pretty much had the sidewalks to himself. Later the dog owners would be out in full force, and the mothers taking their children to school. His route was a long oval leading first north and then west, and there were schools galore to the west.

When Micah went on his runs he never wore his glasses. He hated to feel them bobbing up and down on his nose, was why. He hated how they grew steamy when he sweated. This was unfortunate, because in the past few years his distance vision had noticeably worsened. Not that he was going blind or anything; it was just that he was getting old, as his optometrist so tactlessly put it. At night the lane markings on the streets were all but invisible, and just last week he had whacked a black spider that turned out to be a tangle of sewing thread. On the homeward stretch this morning, he made his usual mistake of imagining for a second that a certain fire hydrant, faded to the pinkish color of an aged clay flowerpot, was a child or a very short grown-up. There was something about the rounded top of it, emerging bit by bit as he descended a slope toward an intersection. Why! he always thought to himself. What was that little redhead doing by the side of the road? Because even though he knew by now that it was only a hydrant, still, for one fleeting instant he had the same delusion all over again, every single morning.

After he had put the hydrant issue behind him he slowed to a walk, panting, and set his hands at his waist in order to get more air in his lungs. He passed the Mission of Kindness and the auto-parts store; he turned onto his own street and passed the lake-trout joint and then took a right up the cracked, stubbled sidewalk leading to his building. A young man in a tan corduroy blazer was sitting on the edge of the stoop—or a boy, really, perhaps not out of his teens. "Hey," he said to Micah, getting to his feet.

"Hey," Micah said. He veered slightly to the left of the boy as he climbed the steps.

"Um," the boy said.

Micah turned to look back at him.

"Do you live here?" the boy asked.

"Yep."

This was a rich kid, Micah saw. Handsome, in that polished and privileged sort of way. Well-cut dark hair conforming to the shape of his skull, collar of his white shirt standing up in back, sleeves of his blazer pushed nearly to his elbows (a style Micah found affected). "Mr. Mortimer?" the boy said.

"Yes?"

"Mr. Micah Mortimer?"

"Yes?"

The boy raised his chin. He said, "I'm Brink Adams."

Wouldn't you know he'd have a name like "Brink."

"Well, hi," Micah said, on a tentative note.

"Brink *Bartell* Adams," the boy said.

Was this supposed to mean something? The boy seemed to think so.

"How do you do," Micah said.

"Lorna Bartell's son."

Micah dropped his hands from his waist. He said, "Whoa." Brink nodded several times.

"Lorna Bartell!" Micah said. "You're kidding. How *is* Lorna, anyway?"

"She's fine."

"Well, what do you know," Micah said. "I haven't thought of Lorna in . . . gosh! What's she up to nowadays?"

"She's a lawyer," Brink said.

Micah said, "Really. Didn't see *that* one coming."

"Why not?" Brink asked, cocking his head. "What did you imagine she'd be doing?"

Micah hadn't given it a thought, to tell the truth. "Oh, well," he said, "the last time I saw her she was not but a, what, a college sophomore, maybe . . ."

"Senior," Brink said.

Actually, no, but Micah didn't bother correcting him. "At any rate, I'm pretty sure she hadn't figured out what she was going to be yet," he said.

Brink still seemed to be waiting for something, but Micah didn't know what. He said, "So! You live around here?"

"No, I'm just passing through," Brink said. "I thought I'd look you up."

"Well, isn't that—"

"You got time for a cup of coffee or something?"

"Uh, sure," Micah said. "You want to come inside?"

"Thanks."

On his own, Micah would have unlocked the front door and headed straight for the basement, but that meant leading Brink through the laundry room and the furnace room, which somehow felt wrong although he couldn't say exactly why. He came back down the steps and took the side path around to the parking lot, with Brink following close behind. "Where's your mom living now?" Micah tossed back as they descended the outside stairwell. His voice gave off a faint echo.

"She's in DC."

"Is that so."

He couldn't remember the name of the town Lorna came from, but it was some little place in western Maryland that she had always planned to go back to after college. She had said she needed mountains around her; she liked how they softened the meeting between the land and the sky. And now look! She was a DC lawyer. Had a son with pushed-up blazer sleeves.

Micah unlocked the back door and stood aside to let Brink enter first. "I'm out of cream, I just want to warn you," he said as they walked into the kitchen.

"That's okay."

Micah gestured toward one of the chairs at the Formica table, and Brink pulled it out and sat down. He was looking toward the living area beyond the kitchen. "Sorry about the mess," Micah said. "I like to get my run out of the way first thing in the morning."

And after that he liked to shower; already he had that itchy feeling down his back as the sweat dried. But he took the ground coffee from the cabinet and started measuring it out. His coffeemaker was an old-style electric percolator that he'd found here when he moved in. The glass knob on its top was wrapped in grayed adhesive tape that kept him from seeing inside, but it still made a good cup of coffee. He filled it with tap water and plugged it in. "You take sugar?" he asked.

"Yes, please."

Micah set the sugar bowl on the table, along with a spoon. He sat down across from Brink.

He saw now that Brink could very well be Lorna's son, in fact, although he wouldn't have guessed it if he hadn't been told. That dark hair (but hers had been long and streaming) and then those eyes, dark also and extra-pointy at the corners like a deer's eyes. His mouth was not Lorna's, though. It was curved at the top, dipping at the center, while hers had been straighter and firmer.

"So," Micah said. "Your mom's a lawyer. What kind of lawyer?"

"She works with Legal Aid."

"Oh. Okay."

In other words, not the high-powered attorney he had been picturing. That made sense. Her family had belonged to some type of fundamentalist church and she had wanted to do good in the world. But it didn't explain the rich-boy son. "How about your dad?" he asked.

"He's a lawyer, too. Corporate."

"Ah."

Micah drummed his fingers absently on the table. The percolator chugged in the background.

"They're both, like, *goal*-oriented," Brink said. "They're

always asking what my plan is. But I don't have a clue what my plan is! I'm just a freshman at Montrose College! And even that is a comedown, as far as they're concerned. They were hoping I'd get into Georgetown, where my dad went. Him especially; seems nothing I do can ever satisfy my dad."

"That's tough," Micah said.

"Him and me are like oil and water," Brink said. "I'm more *your* type of person."

"Me?" Micah was puzzled. "What do you know about my type?"

"You're just an odd-jobs guy. You don't have a dedicated profession."

Great: he had become a poster boy for layabouts. "How do you know that?" he asked Brink.

"My mom said."

Lorna kept track of what he was doing nowadays? Micah blinked.

"I found your photo in a shoebox," Brink said, "along with some others from her college days. Her and you were standing under a dogwood tree and you had your arm around her. So I took it to her and asked, 'Who's this?' and she said, 'Oh! It's Micah. Micah Mortimer,' she said, and then she said you were the love of her life."

"She said that?" Micah asked.

"Well, or she'd thought so at the time, she said."

"Oh."

"I asked where you were now and she said the last she'd heard, you were some sort of computer guru over in Baltimore. My aunt Marissa told her."

"Aunt . . . oh," Micah said. That would be Marissa Baird, he supposed—Lorna's college roommate.

"Mom said she gathered you'd had kind of a checkered career, though, so she didn't know if you were still doing that."

The percolator started its final frenzy of gurgles that meant the coffee was almost ready. Micah stood up and went to take two mugs from the overhead cabinet. He waited until the gurgles had stopped and then filled the mugs and brought them back to the table.

"Aunt Marissa still goes to all their college reunions," Brink said. "She knows where *everyone* is."

"Figures," Micah said.

He slid the sugar bowl toward Brink.

"You weren't very hard to track down," Brink told him.

"No, I don't suppose I was," Micah said.

"'Micah Mortimer, Prop.' Like one of those general-store signs in a Wild West movie, right? Cool!"

"Thanks," Micah said drily.

He took a swallow of coffee. He looked at the bar of sunshine on the floor. The little bit of light that made it through the window above the sink always arrived in the form of a horizontal stripe.

"Question is," he said, "why you would *want* to track me down."

Brink was stirring sugar into his coffee, but he stopped and raised his eyes to Micah. "Look," he said. "You can see I don't belong in that family. I'm a, like, misfit. They're all so . . . I'm more like you."

"But you don't even know me," Micah said.

"Genes do count for *something*, though," Brink said, gazing at him steadily.

"Genes?"

Brink was silent.

"I don't understand," Micah said finally.

"I think you would if you thought about it," Brink said.

"Excuse me?"

Brink released an exasperated puff of a breath. "Do I have to spell it out?" he asked Micah. "You and my mom . . . You two were this item . . . Mom gets pregnant—"

"*What?*"

Brink continued gazing at him.

"Surely your mom isn't saying *I* had anything to do with that," Micah said.

"Mom isn't saying anything. She never has. Any time I've asked who it was, she says it's immaterial."

"Immaterial," Micah said.

He felt an impulse to laugh, but he didn't want to be unkind. "Okay, let's think about this for a sec," he said. "How old are you, anyway?"

"Eighteen," Brink said.

"Eighteen years old. And I left school over twenty years ago—*more* than twenty years ago. By that time your mom and I weren't even together anymore; hadn't seen each other in months. Besides which—"

Besides which, he and Lorna had never once had sex. Lorna wore a special gold ring from her church that meant she was "saving herself," as she put it, and Micah hadn't tried to change her mind. He had sort of admired her absoluteness, you might say. Oh, a lot of Lorna's appeal had been her absoluteness! However, this was probably something he shouldn't get into with her son.

Who was staring at him blankly now. His face had a kind of frozen look. "Well, that's . . ." he said. "Wait; that's not possible."

"Why not?" Micah asked.

"You can tell me the truth, you know," Brink said. "It's not like I'm planning to sue you for child support or anything. I've already *got* a dad. Who legally adopted me, by the way, when him and Mom got married. I'm not expecting anything from you."

"Maybe your dad is your father," Micah said. "Your biological father, I mean."

"No, Mom didn't even meet him until I was two."

"Oh."

Brink was looking angry now. It seemed he'd made a conscious decision to be angry; he suddenly pushed his mug away. A dollop of coffee splashed onto the table. "It *was* you," he said. "Who else could it be?"

"That I couldn't say," Micah told him.

"You were the only boyfriend-type guy in the shoebox."

"Look," Micah said. "I didn't even know she got pregnant. *She's* who you should be asking."

Brink was still glaring at Micah. "I've asked a million times," he said. "She just says all that counts is Dad was the one who helped raise me."

"She's got a point," Micah said.

"But what about my genetic makeup? What if I need to know about some medical condition that runs in that side of the family?"

"Well, if it's any comfort, there are no medical conditions in *my* family that I know of," Micah said.

He'd meant to lighten the atmosphere, but from the expression on Brink's face he saw he'd made a mistake. "Only kidding," he said. "Can I top off your coffee?"

Brink shook his head.

On the kitchen counter, Micah's cell phone rang. He stood up and went over to peer at the screen. It was an unfamiliar number. He unplugged the phone from its charger and answered it. "Tech Hermit," he said.

"Is this Micah Mortimer?"

"Yes."

"Oh, thank God. You're a difficult man to track down. You probably don't remember me; my name's Keith Wayne, and you helped me out some years ago when you were with Computer-Master. Well, I've stopped using Computer-Master; they don't know beans, I've learned . . ."

He paused, perhaps to let Micah chime in and agree with him. Micah actually did not agree; Computer-Master was the first place he'd been hired, and he'd learned a lot there. But he'd left because the boss was a jerk—the type who began his sentences with "Listen here" and "Look, buddy"— so he stayed silent, and eventually Mr. Wayne picked up where he had trailed off. "And now I find myself in an emergency situation," he said. "I've lost every single thing on my computer. Documents, tax files—everything."

"Was it backed up?"

"Well, see, I know I *should* have backed up . . ."

Micah sighed and reached for the notepad beside the toaster. "Okay," he said, "where you located?"

The man lived in Rodgers Forge. Micah told him he'd be there by eleven. Secretly, he was glad to have an excuse to get moving. After he hung up he told Brink, "Looks like I'll need to see to this."

Brink nodded and rose to his feet, not meeting Micah's eyes. He didn't seem angry anymore, just dejected. As he headed for the door, he said, "Well, anyhow, thanks for the coffee."

"Try asking your mom again, hear?" Micah called after him.

Brink just lifted one hand and let it flop as he walked out the door.

"And tell her I said hello!" Micah added, like an idiot. But the door was already closing again with a quiet, conclusive click.

Micah stood motionless for maybe a full minute before he gave his shoulders a shake and went off to take his shower.

Mr. Wayne's lost files were merely in hiding, it turned out. Micah located them in no time, and Mr. Wayne was abjectly grateful. "*However* . . ." Micah said sternly, and Mr. Wayne raised both palms and said, "I know! I know! I've learned my lesson: from now on I'm backing up."

Micah should have asked him how he planned to do that. Chances were he had no notion how. Then Micah could have explained the options and maybe set something up for him, which would have added significantly to the minimum fee he'd just earned. But his heart wasn't in it, somehow. He seemed to be experiencing a nagging sense of something left undone, or done poorly, and so he just said, "Well, you've got my number if you need me," and made his escape.

It was the boy, he thought as he drove down Charles Street. That boy Brink was still tugging at his mind. Clearly he'd been going through a crisis of some kind, and yet Micah had more or less thrown him out. In hindsight he felt guilty about that, partly for Brink's sake and partly for Lorna's, because even after all these years he still thought of Lorna fondly. Or *once again* thought of her fondly, was more like it. (Their breakup had been an angry one; he'd caught her kissing another guy.) But she was his first real love, after all. He had never had much experience with girls. He'd been considered sort of a loner.

When they met he was a junior and she was a brand-new freshman, eating on her own in the cafeteria while the other girls sat in squealing, giggling groups at nearby tables. Her veil of dark hair and her thin face, completely bare of makeup; her pale blouse and faded skirt with their overlaundered look—everything spoke of a certain set-apartness. Yet there was nothing shy or humble about her. She seemed eerily self-contained. He set his tray on her table and asked, "Okay if I sit here?" and she said, "It's fine," without a trace of a smile. He'd liked how she hadn't amped herself up at the sight of him. No sudden flash of teeth or zippy tone of voice. She was who she was. A purist, was how she had struck him. He was intrigued.

In view of her fundamentalist upbringing, it was no surprise now to hear she hadn't ended her pregnancy. The surprise was that she'd gotten pregnant in the first place. Lorna Bartell, so very, very sure of her principles! He never would have believed it.

The panel truck just ahead sped straight through an

amber light, but Micah was prepared and came to a gradual, elegant stop. ("Did you see that?" Traffic God marveled. "Not even the tiniest jolt.")

The thing about old girlfriends, Micah reflected, is that each one subtracts something from you. You say goodbye to your first great romance and move on to the next, but you find you have less to give to the next. A little chip of you has gone missing; you're not quite so wholly *there* in the new relationship. And less there in the one after that, and even less in the one after that one. After Lorna, he'd dated Zara—exotic and dramatic, given to kente-cloth headdresses. And after Zara left him for a fellow dancer, he had taken up with Adele, who'd turned out to be consumed by a passion for animal conservation. One day she had announced that she was heading off to work with gray wolves in the wilds of Montana. Or maybe it was Wyoming. Oh, Micah had not had a very good history with women. It just seemed they kept losing interest in him; he couldn't say exactly why. Now there was Cass, of course, but things certainly weren't the way they had been in the old days with Lorna. With Cass things were more . . . muted. Lower-key. Calmer. And certainly there was no talk of marriage. If Micah had learned anything from all those previous girlfriends, it was that living with someone full-time was just too messy.

He cut over to York Road to pick up a wall switch at Ace Hardware. Also, while he was at it, a set of grab bars for the bathroom in 3B. Then he stopped by the Giant to get the ingredients for his chili.

Pushing his cart past the canned goods, he had a kind of flashback to this morning's dream. The baby had been smack in the middle of an aisle much like this one. It had held itself straight-backed and resolute, the way babies tend to do when they've just recently learned how to sit. Where the devil had that dream come from?

Some might call it prophetic, even if Brink *was* well past infancy.

Back home, he returned the emptied garbage bins to the rear of the building. Then he went into his office and added the wall switch and the grab bars to the list of out-of-pocket expenses he kept for the building's owner. Except he called the grab bars a "replacement towel rod," because grab bars were discretionary items and theoretically the tenants themselves—the Carters—should have been the ones to pay for them. However, Luella Carter had cancer and was getting progressively weaker and more prone to falling. It wasn't as if she'd asked for a spa showerhead or something, Micah reasoned.

Mr. Gerard, the owner, was eighty-some years old and kind of a tightwad, but he lived in Florida now and he didn't interfere all that much.

After lunch three calls came in, one of which was fairly entertaining. A client wanted his teenage son's laptop stripped of its many porn files and outfitted with blocking software. Micah got a kick out of the titles the son had given the files: *Sorghum Production in the Eastern States, Population Figures Dayton Ohio* . . . They reminded him of those hollowed-out books designed to hide people's valuables, always with the driest possible titles imprinted on the spines so outsiders weren't tempted to open them.

The boy's father was from some other country, someplace Asian. Like many of Micah's male clients, he turned out to be the type who liked to hang around and talk tech while Micah was working. First he asked Micah about laser printers versus inkjets, and then about the privacy issues posed by smart-home devices. Micah responded in monosyllables. He preferred to focus on one thing at a time. But it hardly mattered; Mr. Feng just liked to talk.

While Micah was filling out his invoice, Mr. Feng said, "You once helped me with a malware problem when you were with Compu-Clinic. I knew you looked familiar."

"Oh, yeah?" Micah said.

"Now you have your own company, is that so?"

"Well, I wouldn't call it a *company*, exactly . . ."

He tore off the top copy and handed it to Mr. Feng, who looked it over with his lips pursed. "I think I won't mention this to my son," he told Micah. "He'll come home and turn on his computer and wonder what's gone wrong, but how can he ask, right? And I won't volunteer a word."

"Good plan," Micah told him.

"Maybe he'll think God did it," Mr. Feng said.

The two of them laughed.

The other jobs weren't so interesting, though. Install a new operating system; configure a new printer. Humdrum stuff that didn't tax Micah's brain.

The name of the boy Lorna kissed was Larry Edwards. Esmond. It came floating into Micah's head as he was driving home from the printer job. Larry Esmond was small and spindly, with a tiny brown snaggle of a beard poking straight out from the center of his chin like something pasted on. He

belonged to Lorna's Bible-study group. On a late fall afternoon Micah was walking across campus to the computer
lab, and he happened to see Lorna and Larry on a bench
beneath an oak tree. At first he thought Lorna was in some
kind of distress and Larry was comforting her, because she
was sitting in a wilted posture with her head bowed, speaking softly in the direction of her lap, and Larry had one arm
along the back of the bench behind her and was nodding
solemnly as he listened. But then he lifted his free hand to
smooth a strand of hair off her face, and she turned to him
and they kissed.

If this had been a scene in a movie—the wronged lover
standing aghast for a moment before striding up, indignant;
the girl springing to her feet in dismay; the callow interloper
rising too and stammering denials and explanations—Micah
would have snorted. Pure melodrama! And nothing to do
with his own life, or with Lorna's. Lorna was such a *faithful*
person. Almost clingy, sometimes—the way she hung on to
his arm with both hands when they were walking together,
the way she begged to come with him any time he mentioned that he was meeting some guys for a beer or heading
to the gym to shoot some baskets.

There it was, though: Lorna and Larry.

But he didn't think Larry was Brink's father. That was just
too huge a stretch of the imagination.

"One teaspoon chili powder, one teaspoon salt, one quar-
ter teaspoon red-pepper flakes," he said as he measured
them into the pot. He always talked to himself when he was

cooking. He took another look at his aged and spattered index card. "Two *dientes de ajo*, crushed." He set two garlic cloves on the cutting board and slammed his cast-iron skillet down on top of them. He lifted the skillet and looked at the garlic cloves. Then he looked at the bottom of the skillet.

Somebody knocked on his back door.

He thought first it was his front door, because that was the one the tenants used—the one in the living area that they could reach from inside the building. But no, this was a faint *tap-tap* on the door next to the sink. It sounded too hesitant to be Cass. He set the skillet down and went over to open the door. Outside he found the boy Brink, teetering slightly from heel to toe with his hands thrust deep in his pockets. The sun was setting now, and it was chilly enough so that he'd finally pulled his blazer sleeves down.

"Hey," he said to Micah.

"Hi there," Micah said.

Brink went on teetering.

"What's up?" Micah asked him.

"Oh, nothing much."

"You want to come in?"

"Sure," Brink said. He shuffled his feet on the mat and then followed Micah into the kitchen.

"Had a good day?" Micah asked him.

"Oh, yeah. I found a library."

"A library," Micah said.

"I went and sat there."

Did he mean he'd spent the whole day sitting there? Micah didn't want to ask; it might open some can of worms he'd rather not get into. He waved toward the kitchen table and said, "Take a seat, why don't you. Want a beer? Or maybe . . . I don't know," he said, because he remembered then that Brink wasn't of age.

But Brink said, "Beer would be good," and Micah didn't argue with him. He took a Natty Boh from the fridge and handed it over. Then he returned to the counter and scraped the mashed garlic into the chili pot. "One onion, chopped," he said. His least favorite part of the process.

Behind him, he heard the *pfft!* of the beer-can tab.

"I was reading this book about the Orioles," Brink said after a moment. "Gosh, they've been playing a *long* time."

"That they have," Micah said.

"Since 1901, if you count when they were the Brewers."

"The *Milwaukee* Brewers?" Micah asked.

"Right."

Micah turned to look at him. Brink was tipping his chair back, cradling his beer can in both hands.

"But, so, they must not have been the Orioles, then," Micah told him.

"No, for that you have to go to 1953."

"Ah."

Micah resumed chopping the onion.

"Their heyday, though, came in the sixties," Brink said.

"Really," Micah said. He scraped the onion into the pot and stirred everything around. Already he could smell that cumin-y smell that reminded him of stale sweat.

"You've really done your research," he told Brink.

"I had some time on my hands," Brink said.

Micah waited until he'd started the ground beef browning

before he spoke again. Then he took another beer from the fridge and sat down in the other chair. "You feel like having supper here?" he asked finally.

"That'd be great!" Brink said. He let his chair tip forward with a thud.

"It's only chili," Micah told him. "And I've got my woman friend coming. Cass."

"Chili would be great!" Brink said. "And I'd love to meet Cass!"

Micah said, "So . . ."

Brink took on a wary look.

"So what's going on here, exactly?" Micah asked.

"Going on?"

"I mean, school's in session now, isn't it? You're not on some kind of fall break or something."

"Not really," Brink said.

Micah popped the tab on his beer. Then he said, "Where *is* Montrose College, anyhow?"

He hated having to ask, but Brink didn't take offense. "It's in Virginia," he said. "Just over the other side of DC."

"You live in a dorm there? Or commute from home."

"Oh, *God*, no. I'm in a dorm. Who would want to commute?"

"Right," Micah said. He took a swig of his beer.

"Speaking of which," Brink said, "I don't suppose you happen to have a spare bed I could maybe crash on."

"Here?" Micah was taken aback.

"Or just a couch, even. Your couch would be fine," Brink said, and he shot a glance toward the living area.

"Well . . . I do have a sort of guest room, I guess," Micah said.

"Great! Cuz it's kind of late now for me to catch a train."

It wasn't even dusk yet. The trains ran till nearly midnight. But Micah didn't point that out. He slid his chair back and stood up to stir the chili. "You got any luggage?" he called over the sizzling sound of the meat.

"No, I . . . wasn't really thinking ahead."

There was a pause. Then, "One can of kidney beans," Micah said, "rinsed and drained."

"Sure smells good," Brink told him.

"I ought to cook the beans from scratch, but for that I'd have had to start earlier."

"Canned beans are fine with *me*," Brink said.

"They're more expensive, though," Micah said.

"Oh."

Micah was cranking the can opener around the rim of the can. He said, "Do you do much cooking yourself?"

"I don't do any cooking."

"Gotcha."

Micah dumped the beans into a sieve and ran cold water over them.

At the back door, Cass's distinctive knock rang out—a brisk *rat-a-tat*. Micah set the sieve in the sink and went to open the door. "Well, hi," he told her, and she said, "Hi yourself," and handed him the leftover cornbread, wrapped now in Saran Wrap. Her cheeks were slightly flushed, and she radiated a clean, pleasantly wintry smell. Her eyes slid past him to Brink.

"Like you to meet Brink Adams," Micah told her. "Son of a friend from my college days. Brink, this is Cass Slade."

"Hey, Cass," Brink said. He had the rich kid's easy, too-confident manner with strangers.

"Brink is taking a day off from school," Micah told Cass. "He goes to Montrose College."

"Oh, Montrose! One of the women I teach with went there," Cass said.

Micah felt disproportionately grateful to her. He said, "You want a beer?"

"Yes, please."

She shucked off her parka, draping it over the back of the other kitchen chair, and took a seat. "Are you having supper with us?" she asked Brink.

"Yep," he said. And then, "I'm going to crash in the guest room."

"Oh?"

She sent Micah a questioning look, and he nodded as he handed her her beer.

"Well," she told Brink after a pause, "you're going to love Micah's chili."

"It smells great."

Another pause.

"So!" Micah said finally. "Guess I'll bring the extra chair in."

The extra chair was in his office, at the computer desk. By the time he'd carried it back to the kitchen, Brink was telling Cass the history of the Orioles. Cass was looking politely interested. "Really!" she said from time to time. Then, "I'm not from Baltimore originally. I didn't know all that."

"Oh, they have a *long* history."

"And do you play baseball yourself, Brink?"

"Nope."

She waited, cocking her head, but Brink didn't elaborate.

Even though Brink was most definitely not his son, Micah had a sudden inkling of how it would feel if he *did* have a son—one who had turned out to be a disappointment. A dud.

But Cass didn't give up easily. While Micah set the table and tossed the salad she pressed gamely on, quizzing Brink about what sports he did play (lacrosse, of course) and what he thought he might major in (no idea). Micah unwrapped the cornbread and distributed it among the three plates. He spooned chili on top of the cornbread and sprinkled it with grated cheddar, and then he took his seat with the others.

Over dinner, Cass moved on to questions about Brink's family. He had a younger brother and sister, he said. The sister was a fourth-grader, which of course gave Cass lots more to ask about. This evening she wore her hair pulled back into a ponytail—not Micah's favorite style; he liked it when she let it hang straight—and it made her seem closer to Brink's age than to Micah's. When Brink told her about his sister's dyslexia she nodded attentively, sympathetically, and her ponytail bounced up and down on the back of her head. Micah didn't see why she had to get so caught up in all this. He preferred it when she was more reserved. When she was attentive to *him*, to be honest.

He pushed his chair back and rose to heat the water for her after-dinner tea. He didn't ask Brink if he wanted any.

After supper they sat in a row on the daybed in Micah's office and watched the evening news. Micah's TV had to share the desk with his computer, just a few feet in front of them because the room was so narrow. "This here is where you'll be sleeping," he told Brink, slapping the daybed, and Brink said, "I'm good with that."

Micah was mildly curious about Brink's political views, but the whole time the announcers were talking, Brink was consulting his cell phone. Micah glanced toward Cass, hoping to exchange a grimace with her, but she remained stubbornly focused on a line of Latino immigrants being herded into a paddy wagon.

Well before the news was finished, though, she stretched her arms above her head and yawned aloud and said, "I should be going, I guess. I'm really beat." Then she said, "Good night, Brink," and he glanced up from his phone and said, "Hmm? Oh. Nice meeting you."

Micah waited till he and Cass were out in the kitchen before he asked, "You don't want to stay over?"

"No," she said, "you have company." And she took her parka from the back of the chair and shrugged herself into it.

"*That* shouldn't change anything," he said. He wrapped his arms around her from behind and tucked his face into her neck, the warm nook of it that seemed especially designed for the point of his nose. "I was hoping for a little cuddle," he murmured.

But she disentangled his arms and moved toward the door. "You never asked about Nan," she tossed back.

"Oh! Nan," he said. "Right. Did you call her?"

"No," she said. She opened the door and stepped out.

"Don't you think you ought to?" he asked.

She turned and gave him a look he couldn't read. "Maybe I should just go live in a car with Deemolay and his grandmother," she said.

"Aw, now," he said, teasing her. "Why do that when you've got a car of your own you can live in?"

But this didn't make her smile. She just closed the door behind her and left him standing alone in the kitchen.

He stared at the blank expanse of the door for a moment, and then he turned and headed back toward his office. He ought to fetch Brink some sheets, he supposed. Then he would relocate to his bedroom. Ordinarily he hung out on the couch and played solitaire on his phone in the evenings, but not tonight. Not with an audience, so to speak. That was the trouble with houseguests: they took over a person's space. They seeped into all the corners.

The image rose up in his mind of the baby in the supermarket, watching him so expectantly. It occurred to him, not for the first time, that prophetic dreams were not much use if their meaning emerged only in hindsight.

3

B RINK, IT SEEMED, had that teenage knack for sleeping late. When Micah set out on his run the next morning, the office door was tightly closed and silent. It was still that way when he got back, and later when he emerged from his shower. He debated what to do if he had to leave on a client call before Brink woke up. Leave anyhow, he supposed. He didn't figure the kid for any kind of felon.

As he was scrambling eggs, he saw a cell phone in a spangled case lying next to the stove. Brink must have spotted Micah's charger at some point the previous evening and made a mental note of it—returned to the kitchen to plug in his phone after Micah went off to his room. This gave Micah an edgy sense of invasion, although of course there was nothing particularly private about a charging cord. He shook the feeling off and dished his eggs out onto a plate.

Darn, he should have fixed bacon. The smell of frying bacon worked better than any alarm clock, in Micah's experience.

Ding! Brink's phone went. A text. It was loud enough to make Micah glance toward the office door again, but still he heard no sounds of stirring. The phone gave its repeat alert two minutes later. Micah sat down with his eggs.

The percolator stopped chugging, and he rose to pour his first cup of coffee. As he sat back down with it, the phone gave another *ding*. "*Es muy misterioso,*" he said aloud. He added cream to his coffee and waited for the repeat.

Over the course of his breakfast, he heard three more texts come in. So while he was running the water to soak his dishes afterward, he picked up the phone and pressed the Home button. A stack of messages appeared, filling the lock screen. *All I ask is tell us you're alive* and *Your father didn't mean it the way it sounded* and *Brink I'm serious get in touch NOW* and . . .

Micah set the phone down again.

"*Es* not so *misterioso* after all," he said. He turned the faucet off.

His own phone stayed stubbornly silent, so after he'd tidied up he collected his tool bucket from the furnace room and climbed the stairs to the first floor. He had his keys with him just in case, but when he pressed 1B's doorbell, Yolanda answered immediately. She was wearing her exercise outfit—loose pants and a Ravens T-shirt—and a peppy-voiced girl on her TV was chanting, "*Up,* two, three, four; *down,* two, three, four . . ."

"Is this a bad time?" Micah asked.

"Oh, God, no," Yolanda said. "Any excuse to quit torturing myself." She crossed the living room to turn the TV off. The sudden quiet made a sharp, almost echoing sound in Micah's ears.

"You been out yet?" she called after him. He was heading down the hall to her closet.

"I've been out," he said.

Her closet was so stuffed with clothes that they sort of exploded at him when he opened the door. He fought his way through a perfumey, stuffy-smelling mass of fabrics to the circuit-breaker box on the rear wall.

"How cold was it?" she asked.

"Nippy," he said, re-emerging. He came back into the living room and started unscrewing the wall plate.

"Darn. I have to take my car in."

"Well, it's not *cold* cold," he said.

There was a pause, during which she watched him disconnect the old switch and fish the new one from his tool bucket. Then, "So," she said. "You didn't ask about my date with the dentist."

"Ah. The dentist," he said.

"Turns out he lives with his mother."

Micah snorted.

"But that's not a *bad* thing, necessarily. It could just mean he's kindhearted."

"Right," Micah said.

"Which is it, anyhow: you're supposed to marry a guy who gets along well with his mother, or with his father?"

"I didn't know it was either one," Micah said.

"I never can remember. And of course you wouldn't want a guy who's *too* attached to his mother."

"Certainly not," Micah said.

He had the wires of the new switch connected now. He pushed it back inside the wall and bent to retrieve the cover plate from the floor beside his tool bucket.

"He did phone her three separate times over the course of the evening," Yolanda said musingly.

"Uh-oh."

"The third time, she told him she was nervous about these noises she was hearing in the yard and she wanted him to come home."

"So did he go?"

"Well, yes."

Micah screwed in the last screw and then went down the hall to slide the circuit breaker on again. When he got back, Yolanda was waiting for him with her mouth pooched out, her arms folded tightly across her chest. "You think I'm a fool," she told him.

"What?"

"You think I'm kidding myself."

Micah flipped the wall switch, and the ceiling light lit up. "Bingo," he said.

"You *do* think I'm kidding myself?"

"I meant, bingo, your switch is working."

"Oh."

He flipped it off again. She seemed to expect him to say more. "Did he at least approve of your teeth?" he asked finally.

For a moment it seemed she wasn't going to answer. She

just went on studying him with her mouth pooched out. But then she dropped her arms and said, "He didn't say. Well, thanks for coming by, hear?"

"You're welcome," he said, and he picked up his tools and left.

When he was halfway down the stairs to the basement, his phone rang and he stopped to dig it out of his pocket. ADA BROCK. His oldest sister, the family's "linker-upper," as his other sisters called her. He answered. "Ada," he said.

"Hi, hon. How you doing?"

"I'm good."

"Well, guess what! You'll never guess in a million years."

"What."

"Joey's getting married."

"What!"

Joey was Ada's youngest—her baby, she always said, although he must be in his twenties by now. He still lived at home (a theme seemed to be developing this morning), and Micah had assumed he was too pudgy and vacant and aimless even to have a casual girlfriend, let alone get married. But no: "He met her in a grocery store *months* ago, it turns out, but he never said word one to us. Remember some months back, when he thought he might try food management?"

"Food management?"

"And I guess they've been dating ever since, but did he happen to mention it? Not a word. And then last night at dinner he tells us, 'Me and Lily want to get married; can I switch out my single bed for a double?' 'Lily?' I said. 'Who's Lily?' and he said, 'Lily's my fiancée.' Like, *duh*, right? 'So I gather,' I tell him, 'but we've never heard her name before.' 'Well, now you have,' he says. Mr. Wise Guy. I mean, isn't that just like a boy? With the girls it's talk, talk, talk all day long; Lord, I could tell you the color of their fellas' underwear, but here's Joey up and springing a totally foreign person on us with no warning whatsoever."

"She's foreign?"

"What? No, she's American."

"But you just said—"

"An *outside* person, I meant. Unknown."

"Ah."

"So can you come to dinner tomorrow night? Bring Cass. Phil is going to make his famous grilled pork."

"Come to dinner because . . . ?"

"To meet Lily, of course. I told Joey to invite her. I said, 'I refuse to wait till your bride is walking down the aisle before I first lay eyes on her.'"

"Am I going to have to go to the wedding?" Micah asked. He disliked weddings; they always felt so crowded.

"Of course you have to go to the wedding. You're family."

"I didn't have to go to Nancy's wedding."

"Nancy isn't married."

"She's not?"

Micah took a moment to adjust to this. Nancy had three children.

"Six p.m.," Ada said. "Bring Cass, because she's so good at drawing people out. I don't know *shit* about this girl and all of a sudden I'm going to be living with her."

"Well," Micah said, "okay. See you later, I guess."

"No guess about it," Ada told him.

He hung up, although she was probably still talking.

When he got back to his apartment, Brink's phone on the kitchen counter was making its dinging sound. He walked over to check it. A new text had arrived: *If I don't hear from you by . . .* For the first time he noticed that the telephone icon at the bottom of the screen bore a little red 24. Twenty-four unanswered calls; Lord above.

He disconnected the charging cord and took the phone with him to the office door, where he knocked heavily three times. No response. The phone gave another *ding*. Micah knocked again and then opened the door onto dimly lit chaos—blazer in a heap on top of the printer, more clothes on the floor, one shoe near the desk and the other near the daybed, which at first glance seemed no more than a tangle of blankets. Wasn't it amazing how an adolescent boy without a stitch of luggage could still mess up a room! Micah strode across to plop the phone down next to Brink's sleeping profile. "Call your mother," he said.

Brink opened his eyes and stared blankly at the phone, just inches from his nose. He groaned and struggled to a sitting position. "Huh?" he said.

Even after a night's sleep his hair retained its perfect shape, but his left cheek was creased from the pillowcase.

"Your mother," Micah said. "Call her."

"What for?"

"Tell her you're okay."

"Mmph," was all Brink said.

Micah waited till Brink had swung his feet to the floor and was sitting on the edge of the daybed, blinking, before he left the room.

In the kitchen, he started a fresh pot of coffee and put two slices of bread in the toaster. Brink emerged from the office and trudged toward the bathroom, wearing boxer shorts and a T-shirt. In less than a minute he reappeared and shuffled back to the office, rummaging through his hair with one hand. The door slammed behind him.

Micah set the table, ostentatiously clattering dishes so he wouldn't seem to be eavesdropping. Not that there was anything to hear. If Brink was actually calling, he was deliberately keeping his voice down. Or else—a new thought— he had chosen to send a text. Or he was ignoring Micah's directive completely; that was always a possibility. In any case, after a while he came back out, mostly dressed now. His shirt had more wrinkles than yesterday and it wasn't tucked in, but the collar still stood up painstakingly in back. He pulled out a chair and sank down on it like a sack of potatoes. He set an elbow on the table so he could support his head with one hand.

Micah could barely remember being that young, and that shattered by a night's sleep.

"Did you call her?" he asked as he filled Brink's cup.

"Yep," Brink said. He lifted his head and reached for the sugar.

"You talked to her?"

"Yep."

Micah set the two slices of toast on Brink's plate. He slid the jam closer to him. Breakfast was going to be toast and

coffee, period, because to tell the truth, this hospitality business was getting kind of old.

It should have been enough for him to know Lorna could
rest easy now, but somehow it wasn't. What had Brink said
to her, exactly? Had he mentioned Micah? And if he had,
what had *she* said? Had she asked how Micah was doing?
No, she couldn't have; the call hadn't lasted long enough.
And why would she care, anyway, after all these years?

Brink piled so much jam on his toast that he had to lift his
upper lip as he took his first bite so as not to get a jam mus-
tache. This gave him a snarling, doglike appearance. Micah,
lounging against the kitchen counter, averted his gaze.

A ringing sound came from one of Brink's pockets. It was
that jingly, old-timey, landline kind of ring, an odd choice
for a kid. Brink went on chewing his toast. The phone went
on ringing. "Don't you want to answer that?" Micah asked
finally.

"Nah," Brink said.

He reached for his coffee and took a sip. He kept his eyes
completely lowered. His lashes were short and stubby but
thick, like an artist's paintbrush.

Come to think of it, a kid might choose that ring for calls
from the grown-ups in his life.

Micah said, "You did get in touch with her, right?"

"*Yes*, I said. What! Don't you trust me?"

Micah straightened up from the counter.

"You didn't," he said.

Brink sighed loudly and sent a gaze toward the ceiling.

"Listen," Micah told him. "I'm not sure what's going on
here, but clearly she's worried about you. It's not going to
kill you just to tell her you're safe, is it?"

"What do *you* know about it?" Brink said. The sudden flash of anger in his voice took Micah by surprise. "I'm sick of being in the wrong all the time! I've had it! I thought you, at least, would see my side of it, but oh, no—right off the bat you're on *their* side, just like everyone else."

"I don't even know what your side *is*," Micah said. "You haven't told me a damn thing."

"Well, did you ask?"

"Okay, I'm asking now. Okay?"

Brink didn't answer. He had his fists clenched at either side of his plate.

"All right," Micah said finally. "I can't force you to talk. And I can't force you to call your mom. But I am sure as hell not going to be your accomplice in this. Either you tell her right now where you are, while I am standing here listening, or you leave."

"Fine; I'll leave," Brink said.

But he stayed seated.

"So go, then," Micah said.

By now, of course, Brink's phone had stopped ringing. There was a pause, and then Brink slid his chair back and stood up. He turned and went into the office while Micah watched, not knowing what to expect. In no time he reappeared, carrying his blazer over his shoulder by one hooked finger, and he headed for the back door. He opened the door and stepped out. "So . . ." Micah said, trailing after him. "So where will you go, do you think?"

Brink didn't answer. The door closed behind him.

Micah came to a halt.

He had handled this all wrong, he realized. But even given a second chance, he wasn't sure what he'd do differently.

. . .

A man in Guilford needed his computer checked for malware. A woman who'd read *First, Plug It In* wanted to know how much he charged for lessons but then said she would have to talk it over with her husband. Another woman needed help installing her new modem. Comcast had sworn she could easily do it herself, she said, "but you know how *that* goes," she added. "Right," Micah said, and sure enough, even he ended up having to call the support line because they'd sent a reconditioned unit still linked to the previous owner, it appeared. He was kept on hold nearly twenty minutes but he didn't charge the client for that because it wasn't her fault. He told her he had checked his email while he was waiting and so it wouldn't count as billable time.

Then there was a blank spell in which he saw to a few random chores. He dusted his apartment—his regular Wednesday task—and stripped the linens off the daybed and started a load of laundry. He raked the leaves that had collected outside the basement windows. He installed the grab bars in the Carters' bathroom.

It was unfortunate that the Carters lived on the third floor, because Luella Carter was too weak now to manage stairs. Her world had shrunk to four rooms, pretty much, and Micah hadn't seen her out of her bathrobe in he didn't know how long. She wasn't all that old, either—just in her late fifties or so, a once-heavy woman gone sunken. She didn't seem to fully realize her situation, though. She tottered into the bathroom to keep him company while he worked, and in between short, effortful breaths of air she gave him a merry description of a recent visit from her knitting group. "We all go *way* back," she told him. "There are six of us, and we don't only knit; we take these outings sometimes. Last spring we toured a pickle factory down on the waterfront, and the manager gave each of us a jar of midget gherkins when we left. They were delicious! Then on Halloween every year we go to this pumpkin farm in Baltimore County and we bring along stuff for a picnic. I cannot wait! We always laugh so hard! Oh, we're a bunch of kooks, I tell you. This year we're planning to buy the teeny kind of pumpkins, the baseball-size kind, because my friend Mimi found this recipe for pumpkin soup served inside hollowed-out pumpkin bowls and they looked so cute! Like something from a magazine."

Micah didn't see how she could possibly hope to attend a picnic out in the county, let alone fix her own soup, but he said, "You going to bring *me* some soup, Luella?" and she laughed and said, "Oh, we'll see. We'll have to see how you behave yourself."

Then Micah started his drill up, but that didn't stop her from talking. When he turned the drill off again she seemed to be discussing herbal teas. "They say chamomile's the best thing for it," she said, and at first he thought she meant the best thing for cancer, but it turned out she meant for insomnia. "You're supposed to drink chamomile just before bed and you will drift right off. So I said to Donnie, I said, 'Fix me a cup tonight and let's find out if it works,' because I'll try anything, I tell you. Anything at all. It makes me *crazy*, not sleeping! I turn on my left side, turn on my right; I puff my pillows up. I listen to Donnie snoring away and it feels like he is tormenting me, like he's saying, 'Look at *me*! *I* can sleep just fine!' But you know what? That tea didn't do a durn thing. First off, it tasted no better than dishpan water, and then on top of that it did not do one thing. All last night I'm laying there, laying there . . . and Donnie is snoring like a motorboat. I tell you, I started getting *angry*. I was angrier than I've ever been in my life, I do believe. Finally I reach over and give Donnie a punch in the shoulder. 'What!' he says. Like, starting up, like. 'I cannot stand this!' I say to him. 'I got to have my rest, I tell you! And there you are, snoring away. I'm so angry I could *spit*!'"

Apparently she had no idea what was really making her angry, but Micah wasn't about to tell her. He just said, "Oh, yeah. It's a bitch all right, not sleeping." And then he started his drill again.

This time, she fell silent while the drill ran. She waited until he had turned it off before she said, "Yesterday my doctor told me, he said, 'Now, Luella,' he said. Said, 'You know this is incurable, don't you?' And I said, 'Yes, I know.'"

Micah lowered his drill and looked over at her.

She said, "I mean, I'm not angry at God, exactly. But I'm angry."

"Well, sure you are," Micah said.

He was ashamed that he had assumed she didn't realize.

Micah composed an email addressed to all the building's tenants, cc'ing Mr. Gerard as usual to prove he was doing his job.

Dear Residents:

    Once again it's my day to set the recycling out, and once again I see that people haven't flattened their cartons. Two large cartons are currently sitting out back in their original, three-dimensional state. With their address labels still attached, by the way, so I know who the culprits are.

This is a city ordinance, folks. It's not some idle whim of mine. The Department of Public Works requires that cartons be broken down before recycling. Please see to it by six p.m. so I won't have to bring in my hit man.

Yours wearily,
Micah

He clicked on Send, and whoosh, off it went. Then he checked the time at the top of his computer screen. 4:45. Cass should have finished work by now. He pulled out his phone and tapped her number.

"Hello, Micah," she said.

"Hi," he said. "You home yet?"

"I just walked in."

"Oh, good. Say!" he said. "Did you ever call Nan?"

He had made a mental note to ask her this, to make up for not asking those other times. He realized he'd been remiss there.

"No," she said. "As it happens, Nan called *me* again."

"Oh, yeah?"

"She said she and Richard have set the date, finally, and so she's giving up the apartment."

"That's great," Micah said.

"Right," Cass said.

There was something wry in her tone that he couldn't read. He said, "You do plan to take over the lease, don't you?"

Cass said, "Oh, yes," but offhandedly, as if she had not been obsessing about the subject for the past several days. Then she said, "How's your house guest?"

"Brink? Oh, he left."

"He's not staying there anymore?"

"Nope," Micah said. "In fact, I feel kind of bad about him."

"Why's that?"

"Well, I basically kicked him out."

"Kicked him out!"

"It seemed he might be, I don't know, running away from home or something. He wouldn't tell his mom his where-abouts, and I felt like he was putting me smack in the middle of things. I said he'd have to get in touch with her or leave, one or the other. So he left."

"Where'd he go?"

"I have no idea," Micah said. "But anyhow! Enough about him. The reason I called is, Ada's asked us to supper tomorrow. The whole family's getting together to meet this girl Joey's engaged to. Can you come?"

"Oh . . . I guess not, Micah," Cass said.

"You guess not?"

She was silent for a moment. "As a matter of fact," she said finally, "I'm wondering if we should stop seeing each other."

Something hit him in the concave place just below his rib cage.

He said, "What? Why?"

"Why do you suppose?" she said. "There I was, on the verge of losing my apartment. I call and tell you I'm about to be homeless. But did you offer me a place to stay?"

"Stay *here*?"

"In fact," Cass said steadily, "what did you do? Quick-quick invite the nearest stranger into your spare room."

"Oh, for God's sake," Micah said.

"Okay, maybe it was subconscious. Maybe you didn't stop to ask yourself why you did it. But face it, Micah: you made very sure to arrange things so it would be awkward for me to move in with you."

"That never even crossed my mind! I didn't even know you were *willing* to move in! Is *that* what this is about? You all at once think we ought to change the rules?"

"No, Micah," she said. "I know that you are you."

"What is *that* supposed to mean?"

"I'm just saying that the you that you are might not be the right you for *me*."

Micah was silent.

"You can see why I would be wondering, right?" she said.

"Well," he said. "I guess there's no point arguing, if that's the way you feel."

Another silence.

"Well . . . okay. So, goodbye, then," she said.

She hung up.

Micah slipped his phone into his pocket and then sat there awhile, doing nothing.

While he was hauling the recycling to the alley that evening, he started getting mad. This was unfair! No, he had *not* engineered Brink's stay, either consciously or unconsciously. And anyhow, so what if the spare room was occupied? Presumably she'd have slept in Micah's room anyhow, in Micah's double bed, the way she always did when she stayed over.

Besides: if she'd wanted to move in with him, why hadn't she just said so? Why was she so quick to break up with him at the first excuse? It was almost as if there were something else she hadn't talked about. She hadn't given him a chance to defend himself.

He hated it when women expected you to read their minds.

He scowled down into 3A's recycling bin, which was overflowing with those transparent plastic clamshell containers that the DPW forbade.

How he and Cass had met:

He'd been on a tech call, one December morning a few years back. A charter school off Harford Road, Linchpin Elementary, was having trouble with the Wi-Fi connection in two of its classrooms, and one of those classrooms was Cass's.

Micah did notice, when she answered his knock, that she was attractive—nearly as tall as he was, with a friendly, open face—but the main thing on his mind right then was installing the booster he'd brought. So straightaway he started traveling around the perimeter of the room, stopping from time to time to consult the signal on his phone app. Meanwhile, Cass—Ms. Slade—stood by her desk discussing something with two little boys. Or *they* were discussing something. She was just listening, tilting her head thoughtfully. "Well," Micah heard her say finally, "I can understand your feelings. However, I don't believe you're considering both sides of this." Then she gave a single clap of her hands, causing the boys to look startled. "Class," she said, raising her voice, "may I have your attention, please?"

The other children, seated at their desks, stopped murmuring among themselves and looked up.

She said, "Travis and Conrad here are not happy about our caroling plan. They think the nursing home is creepy."

"It's got this *smell*," either Travis or Conrad clarified.

"They feel it smells bad," she translated for the others.

"And the old ladies keep reaching out to us with their clutchy, grabby hands."

"When we went last year in third grade," the other boy said, "one of them kissed me on the face."

So far the rest of the class had listened in silence, but now several of them said, "Eww!"

"However," Cass announced in her ringing voice, "I'd like you to look at this from another angle. Some of those people get to see children only once a year at Christmas, when our school comes to carol. And even the grown-ups they knew are mostly gone. Their parents are gone, their friends are gone, their husbands or wives gone—whole *worlds* gone. Even their brothers and sisters, often. They remember something that happened when they were, say, nine years old—same age as you all are now—but nobody else alive remembers it too. You don't think that's hard? You'll be singing to a roomful of broken hearts, I tell you. Try thinking of that when you decide you don't want to bother doing it."

Ridiculously, Micah had felt touched, although in his own experience most old people were relentlessly cheery. The children seemed unmoved, however. Several of them were speaking up to disagree. "They can't even hear us, though! They're wearing those skin-colored hearing aids!" and "Why would it make them feel better to see kids they don't know from Adam?"

Cass clapped her hands again. "All right, now, simmer down," she said. "Whoever feels strongly about this can just not go with us, okay? I'll ask Ms. Knight if you can spend that time in the library. Who would like to do that? Anyone? Anyone?"

But none of them volunteered, not even Travis or Conrad.

"Well, then," she said. She turned to take a book from her desk. "Let's all look at page eighty-six."

The children started rustling pages, and Travis and Conrad went back to their seats, and Micah plugged his booster into an outlet and watched for the orange light to come on.

He'd had to show Cass how to work things, of course, once he was finished. During the next lull, while a little girl was industriously solving a math problem on the blackboard, he crooked an index finger at Cass and she came over to him. "So," he said in a low voice, "this here is the name of your booster's Wi-Fi signal, see?" and he pointed it out on his phone screen. "Same password you've used before, but the name has this extra extension now."

Cass nodded, her eyes on the screen. She smelled like toothpaste.

"Do you like going to movies?" he asked suddenly.

She sent him a surprised look.

"It's just that I thought you might want to see something at the Charles with me," he said. (The Charles tended toward classier titles, not just slapstick or shoot-'em-ups.) "I mean, unless you're married or something."

"No," she said.

As soon as the word was out of her mouth, Micah resigned himself. But then she said, "I'm not married."

She searched his face for a moment. She seemed to be try-ing to make up her mind about him. Micah stood straighter and pulled his stomach in.

"And I do like going to movies," she said. "I mean, depend-ing on what's playing."

"Well, then," he told her. And he couldn't keep from grinning.

It was her speech to the children that had won him. "A roomful of broken hearts"! He liked that phrase.

But now look.

Neither of the two recycling offenders had come out to flatten their cartons. Neither Ed Allen in 1A or Mr. Lane in 2B—outlaws, both of them. Micah laid the first carton down on its side and stamped on it. He didn't open the end flaps first; he just stamped on it till it collapsed. Stamp, stamp, stamp.

4

ADA AND HER FAMILY lived in Hampden. The houses on their block were small and plain but extremely well cared for, because most of the inhabitants were carpenters or plumbers or such and they had their standards. Unfortunately, though, the streets nearby had started filling up with fancy new restaurants and la-di-da boutiques, and this meant a sudden traffic problem throughout the neighborhood. Micah had to hunt awhile for parking, and he ended up in a questionable spot where his rear bumper protruded a teeny bit into an alley. So he was feeling a little distracted when he arrived at the house.

The yard here was not much bigger than two doormats, one on either side of the walkway, and Ada's husband kept it meticulously maintained, the grass mown down to mere fuzz and not a single autumn leaf floating in the fiberglass birdbath. But Ada, like all of Micah's sisters, had a boundless tolerance for clutter. Micah had to swerve around a skateboard and a sippy cup on his way up the front steps, and the porch was strewn not only with the standard strollers and tricycles but also with a pair of snow boots from last winter, a paper bag full of coat hangers, and what appeared to be somebody's breakfast plate bearing a wrung-out half of a grapefruit.

In the foyer (which he entered without knocking; nobody ever knocked, and anyhow, it wouldn't have been heard in all the ruckus), so many sneakers lay heaped on the floor that you would think the house had a no-shoes rule, although it didn't. A mahogany side table held a lamp and a pair of pruning shears and a bottle of nail polish. No doubt the living room was equally disorganized, but you couldn't tell, because it was filled wall-to-wall with people. His twin sisters, Liz and Norma (who looked nothing alike—one thin and one fat), were making a fuss over Ada's youngest grandson; and Liz's husband, Kegger, was talking on his cell phone near the window; and a couchful of teenagers sat watching a game of some kind on the giant flat-screen TV. Micah didn't see Joey or any bride-to-be type of person, but maybe they were lost in the crowd. The general impression, as always, was tumult: noisy, merry, unkempt people wearing wild colors, dog barking, baby crying, TV blaring, bowls of chips and dips already savaged.

Ada's husband was the first to notice Micah. He was a burly, gray-bearded man with a denim apron strained tight across his beachball stomach, and he appeared in the dining-room doorway holding a foot-and-a-half-long spatula. "Bro!" he shouted. "High time you got here!" Behind him came Ada, big-boned and brightly lipsticked beneath a frizz of dyed red hair, bearing a magnum of chardonnay. "Hey, hon!" she said. "Where's Cass?"

"Oh, she . . . had another engagement," he said.

"Well, shoot. You want some wine?"

"I'll get myself a beer," he said. "Where's the happy couple?"

She turned to scan the crowd. "Joey must be out back," she said. "Oh, but, Lily! Come over here, sweetie!" She was speaking to a pale young towheaded girl whom Micah hadn't noticed before. "Like you to meet my baby brother, Micah."

"How do you do," Lily said, and she approached holding her hand out dutifully, like a child minding her manners.

"Hey there, Lily," Micah said.

Her hand was small and very cold. She wore plastic-rimmed cat's-eye glasses and a great deal of jewelry—chandelier earrings, rhinestone barrettes, bangle bracelets, a double strand of beads as well as a large oval brooch, everything in some shade of blue to go with her dressy blue dress. Micah had the impression that this was the first time she'd been out on her own among grown-ups.

"Lily works at Grocery Heaven," Ada said. "You know that Grocery Heaven out on Belair Road."

"Ah, yes," Micah said.

"*Organic* outfit," Phil said in a weighty tone. "Hippie stuff. Granola."

"Do you ever shop there?" Lily asked Micah.

"No, I . . . That's kind of out of my way."

"Well, I'm at the Customer Care counter, if you happen to stop by sometime."

"So that's how you met Joey?"

"Yes, Joey tried working in produce awhile, but I don't think food management turned out to be his thing."

"I stayed just long enough to ask Lily out for a burger," Joey said, materializing next to her. He set an arm around her shoulders and asked Micah, "Don't I know how to pick 'em?"

"You're a lucky man, all right," Micah said. He was thinking that Joey—pink-faced and chubby, wearing a sweat suit and purple Crocs—seemed dressed for a whole different occasion from the one Lily had dressed for. But she beamed up at him adoringly and let him pull her sideways against him.

"Uncle Micah's an IT guy," Joey told her. "He's got his own company and all."

"Oh, *you* could do that, Joey, honey!" Lily said.

This implied that Joey had still not found his chosen line of work, which was a troubling thought if he was about to get married. But Joey smiled confidently and said, "Sure! I could do that."

Someone pushed a cold beer can into Micah's hand—Suze, the youngest of his sisters and the one he felt closest to. "Did you not bring Cass?" she asked him.

"She had something to do," Micah said. And then—because he might as well get it over with—"In fact, I think we've broken up."

"Broken up!" Suze said.

The words cut through the babble like a knife. Everyone fell magically silent and looked at him.

"But we *loved* Cass!" Ada said. "You are never, ever again going to find anyone else as right for you!"

Micah said, "Gee, that's a comfort to hear."

"Durn, I wanted Lily to meet her," Joey said. And then, turning to Lily, "You'd have been crazy about her."

"Oh, well," Micah said. "These things happen."

Someone on the TV was announcing a substitution—"Going to bring in Hawkins to replace the injured Kratowsky"—but the teenagers on the couch were all watching Micah instead. One of them—Norma's daughter, Amy—said, "She was going to help me with my college application!"

"You're applying to college?" Micah asked her.

It didn't work. Everyone went on staring at him.

"Could you not try to get her back?" Ada asked. (Wouldn't you know that she would assume the breakup was Cass's idea.)

And "Tell her you'll change your ways," Phil advised him.

"Change what ways?" Micah asked.

This made them all start laughing; he didn't know why. Nor did Lily, of course. She looked from him to the others, and then at him again. Joey told her, "Uncle Micah's kind of . . . finicky."

"I am not *finicky*," Micah said.

"What day is it today, Micah?" Suze's husband called from the foyer doorway. He had a small child on his shoulders; her flounced skirt encircled his neck like an Elizabethan ruff.

"What do you mean, what day? It's Thursday."

"Is it vacuuming day? Is it dusting day? Is it scrub-the-baseboards-with-a-Q-tip day?"

"Oh, Dave, leave him alone," Suze said.

"He doesn't mind! Is it window-washing day?"

"Well," Micah said grudgingly, "it's kitchen day, as it happens."

"Kitchen day! Ha! Your kitchen has a day all its own?"

"Yes."

"And what does that involve, exactly?"

"For God's sake, Dave," Ada said. She set an arm protectively around Micah's waist.

"What?" Dave said. "I'm only trying to understand, is all. What on earth needs doing in his kitchen? Any time I've seen it, we could eat off the floor."

"It's not *floor*-mopping day," Micah said. "It's kitchen day. On kitchen day I clean the counters and the appliances and such. And one complete cabinet."

"One cabinet?"

"In rotation."

They laughed again, and Micah gave an exaggerated scowl. He wasn't sure why he played along with them like this. (Even encouraged them, some might say.)

Suze said, "Never you mind, Micah. We're just going to pretend my husband has some manners. Teasing a man when his girlfriend has ditched him! Ada, is it not time to eat yet? Let's have supper!"

"Yes, come to the dining room, everyone," Ada said, and she let go of Micah and turned to lead the way. "When Robby needed help with his reading," she told Lily, "—that's Nancy's oldest, my grandson—Cass stepped right up to help. She's a teacher, you know. We worried Robby might have a learning disability, but Cass was so patient with him! And that was all he needed, it turned out. Oh, everyone thought the world of her."

Micah felt an unexpected flash of resentment. Cass wasn't perfect, for pity's sake! She could have just let him know straight out if something was bothering her, instead of brooding about it in silence. And anyhow, shouldn't his family be on *his* side, here?

Ada's dining-room sideboard was loaded with food—Phil's grilled pork, and mac 'n' cheese for the little ones and the teenage-girl vegetarians, and green salad and potato salad and sautéed squash and string-bean casserole. (Also a flashlight, a *People* magazine, and a vase of dead chrysanthemums, but never mind.) The table itself was bare, except for a portable Ping-Pong net that had been stretched across the center for the past couple of years or so—long enough, at any rate, so that everyone had stopped seeing it. There were no place settings, because the custom was that the young people ate in the living room while the grown-ups crammed helter-skelter around the dining-room table on a jumble of chairs and stools and benches. "Now, Lily, honey, you sit at the head, you and Joey both," Ada said. "Joey? Where's Joey? You get back in here, Joey!" because Joey was already following the teenagers to the living room. "You're sitting next to Lily, hear?"

Micah took his own plate and silver to a spot along the side, in the middle of a row of temporarily empty seats. He set the silver to his left, on account of the Ping-Pong net on his right. "When's the wedding?" he asked Lily.

"Well, I was thinking Christmas," she said, "but Joey doesn't want to combine it with a holiday."

"I say we deserve a separate set of days off," Joey told Micah. "One set of days for Christmas and another set for the wedding."

"Days off from what?" Micah asked.

"Huh?"

"Where are you working now?"

"Oh. I'm not. I'm just looking around, at the moment," Joey said cheerfully. "But I *will* be working, come Christmas."

"If it's Christmas, we could have a red-and-green theme for the shower," Ada said. "I am giving the bridal shower," she told Micah. "Me and the twins together. Nowadays showers are coed; did you know that? You can come too."

"Oh, ah . . ."

"Remember, Ada?" Suze called from the other end of the table. "Remember *my* shower?"

Everyone hooted, and Ada grimaced. "That was a Fourth of July theme," she told Lily. "Sparklers stuck in vases, and sparklers on the cakes. So this spark lands on one of the placemats and starts a teeny fire, and the smoke alarm goes off and the fire department shows up, but *we* didn't know; we had unplugged the alarm and we thought that had done the trick. We thought the firemen were only dressed as firemen and so some of the gals shouted, 'Take it off! Take it *all* off!' thinking they were strippers that maybe one of the guys had sent, till the firemen said, 'Sorry, ladies; hate to disappoint you—'"

"—which would never happen at a coed shower," a daughter-in-law put in.

Lily looked relieved.

"The color scheme of course was patriotic," Norma said in a reminiscent tone. "Right, hon?" she called down the table to her husband. "Grant was clerking at Read's back then," she told Lily. "He got us a special deal on red-white-and-blue decorations."

"And Liz came in shorts, because she thought it would be, like, a Fourth of July cookout," Ada said. "But it wasn't a cookout! It was dressy! Dressed-up gals are walking up the sidewalk! So when she sees that, she gets a pleated skirt out of a dry-cleaner's bag that's hanging in her car and she holds it up to her waist and sashays on into the party, skirt swishing in front of her and bare legs showing in back."

All the women hooted again, and Lily gave a tentative smile.

"Great job on the pork, Phil," Micah said. He was wondering if he'd be offered some leftovers to take home.

"Thanks," Phil said. "I used these special new kind of briquets they sell at Home Depot now. Not exactly what you'd call cheap: fourteen ninety-eight for a dinky little . . ."

This was interesting to the men but not the women, who turned away and began stirring among themselves. The four sisters—lifelong waitresses, all of them—rose in a group to top off glasses and offer condiments, traveling around the table with various bowls from the sideboard. "Kids?" one called toward the living room. "Anybody need anything?" A couple of the little ones straggled back into the dining room to climb on their mothers' laps. "*Somebody* missed her nap today," a daughter-in-law told her husband over a toddler's head. Meanwhile the sisters were asking, "Who's for a biscuit?" and "Anybody prefer well-done?" and a long pair of tongs appeared above Micah's left shoulder to drop another slice of pork onto his plate.

Micah always thought that *of course* his sisters would choose to be waitresses. Restaurants had the same atmosphere of catastrophe that prevailed in their own homes, with pots clanking and glassware clashing and people shouting "Coming through!" and "Watch your head!" and "Help! I'm in the weeds!" A battlefield atmosphere, basically.

Kegger, across the table from Micah, cleared his throat. "So. Mikey," he said.

Micah sprinkled salt on his meat.

"Mikey?"

Micah cut himself a bite-size chunk and speared it with his fork.

"Kegger is speaking to you, Micah," Ada said.

He looked up. "Oh, yeah?" he said. "Funny; I didn't hear my name."

"My-*kah*," Kegger corrected himself.

"Yes, Kegger?" Micah said.

"I'm thinking of buying a new computer. Like to ask you a few questions."

Now the other men turned toward Micah. They loved talking tech. It was even more fun than comparing driving routes.

"Am I better off getting a Mac? I'm thinking maybe so. But I don't know squat about Macs! I don't even know what model I want."

"I can help you with that," Micah said. He popped the chunk of meat into his mouth.

"You can?"

Micah was chewing now.

"You got a catalog or something?"

"I'll meet you at the Apple Store and take you through the options," Micah said once he'd swallowed. "That's what I do with my clients."

"That would be great," Kegger said. "Of course I'm willing to pay for your time, you understand," he added unconvincingly.

"Nah," Micah said.

He'd long ago resigned himself to helping family members for free. In a way, it let him off the hook. It made them think he wasn't such a weirdo after all. Although not *entirely* off the hook, because just when it seemed that his sisters had forgotten all about the Cass discussion, Liz returned to it. "One reason I thought Cass was so good for you," she said as she settled back into her seat, "is that she was the eentsiest little bit finicky herself."

"It's true," Ada said. "She always liked for her purse to be the exact same color as her shoes."

"What's finicky about that?" Micah wondered.

"Aha! See there? You're sticking up for her."

"I'm not—"

"Also," Liz said, "she practically never went to visit her brother who lived in California, because it was three hours later there and she hated to change her bedtime."

"So how she could dump Micah just on account of cuz he cleans his kitchen on Thursdays—" Ada said.

"That's not why she dumped me!" Micah said.

"Why, then?"

Everyone waited for his answer. Even the men looked interested.

"Well, as near as I can tell," Micah said, "she's mad because I let this kid sleep in my guest room."

"What? What kid?"

"This son of an old girlfriend," Micah said.

"Which old girlfriend?"

"Oh . . . you-all remember Lorna."

"Lorna *Bartell*?"

Micah never could get over how his sisters appeared to retain every personal detail about everyone they'd ever met. Shouldn't they be periodically clearing out their memory caches or something? It must be twenty-odd years since they had last laid eyes on Lorna—and just once or twice, even then, when he'd brought her to Thanksgiving dinner and such—but all four of them sat up sharply, and Suze said, "The Lorna who two-timed you junior year? *That* Lorna? How dare she ask you to put her son up?"

"She didn't—sheesh!" Micah said. He was sorry now that he'd mentioned her. "Lorna didn't know anything about it. The kid was just, like, playing hooky from school or whatever, and he wanted a bed for the night and I told him sure. Lorna had no idea! In fact, she kept texting him and asking where he was."

There was a silence. For once, his sisters seemed at a loss for words. "So . . ." Suze said finally. "So, let me see if I'm following this. Cass broke up with you because you gave your guest room to the son of an ex-girlfriend that you don't even see anymore, that you haven't been in touch with since college."

"No, it was because I gave my guest room to *anyone*. Period. It had nothing to do with who his mother happened to be."

"Want to bet?" Liz asked.

"Honest; she didn't even know about his mother."

They studied him, all wearing the same dubious expression.

"See, Cass thought she was about to lose her apartment,"

Micah told them finally. "She didn't, as it turned out, but for a while there she was thinking she was going to end up homeless. And somehow she got it into her head that the minute I heard about it, I quick installed a kid in my guest room just to keep her from moving in with me."

"Well, that's ridiculous," Ada said after she had absorbed this.

"Right. Now you have it," Micah said. "She did admit that, okay, maybe my motive had been subconscious, but even so—"

"Subconscious. I despise that word," Phil told his brothers-in-law.

"All that psych shit," Kegger agreed.

"And we're talking about just the guest room!" Micah said. "Where she wouldn't even be staying! The guest room had nothing to *do* with whether she could move in."

"Whole thing makes no sense," Phil said, tipping his chair back.

"Also," Micah said, "how does she explain the fact that I kicked him out after one night, hmm? If she *had* been evicted, he'd have been gone before she got there. How about *that*, I want to know."

"You kicked him out?" Liz asked.

"Well, so to speak."

"How come?"

"I told him he needed to let his mother know where he was. She was just calling him and calling, texting him and texting, wondering if he was all right. It put me in the middle of things. So when he wouldn't answer her, I made him leave."

"Oh, it's *cruel* not to tell his mother," Norma said.

Ada rose to clear the table, layering plates in a professional way along the length of her forearm and heading off to the kitchen, but her sisters seemed too transfixed by Micah's story to help her. "I always did think Lorna Bartell was kind of a . . . minnow of a person," Liz told him. "Not the right type for you at all. But even so, she deserves to know her son's whereabouts."

"Well, Brink would not agree with you," Micah said. "He just up and walked out."

"*Brink*, his name is?"

"Yep."

"He play lacrosse?" Kegger asked.

"Yep."

Kegger nodded, looking satisfied. "Preppy," he told Phil. "Wears loafers without any socks."

"Well, actually he wore—"

"And then what did *you* do?" Ada asked Micah, returning from the kitchen.

"Me?"

"Did *you* tell his mom where he is?"

"Well, no."

"Why not?"

"I don't even know where he is, at the moment. And besides, I wouldn't have a clue how to reach her."

Ada removed his plate but went on standing at his elbow, frowning down at him. "We *are* in the modern age," she said.

"What's that got to do with it?"

"Does she live here in Baltimore?"

"No, she does not. She's in DC, as it happens."

"So? Have you looked up her number?"

"I don't want to call her! I'm a total stranger by now."

"What'd you say her last name was? Bartell?" Phil asked. "She still got her same last name?" He had taken his cell phone out and he was stabbing it with his index finger.

"Nobody on earth lists their phone number anymore," Micah told him.

"Is she on Facebook?"

"Not if she's in her right mind she's not."

"I don't know how you can say that," Suze told him. "If I weren't on Facebook, I wouldn't know what a single high-school friend of mine was up to."

"You care what your high-school friends are up to?" Micah asked.

Liz's teenage son, Carl, wearing a cast on his left arm, appeared in the living-room doorway. "When's dessert?" he asked.

"When everybody's dishes are brought in from the living room," Liz told him.

"*What* is dessert?"

"Wait-and-see pudding."

"Aw, Ma . . ." He went back to the living room.

"How come the cast?" Micah asked, but nobody answered. Ada left for the kitchen with another few plates, and Phil, who was still scrolling through something on his phone, asked, "Does Lorna work, do you happen to know? It would help if we had the name of an employer."

"There is no point in me calling her up just to say I don't know where her son is," Micah told him.

"You know he's alive, though," Liz said. "You know he's traveling of his own free will. Lorna might be thinking he's been kidnapped! Oh, no one should have to go through that, not even Lorna Bartell. Sitting there just helpless wondering if her child's lying dead on the side of the road."

"He's not exactly a child," Micah said. And then, persisting, "Why is Carl's arm in a cast?"

"Because he's an idiot," Liz said. She had risen, finally, to clear the dishes from the sideboard. She paused with a casserole clutched to her midriff and said, "Him and his pals, it seems, were delivering a mattress to this one guy's rec room. I don't know what they wanted with somebody's hand-me-down mattress, or rather I don't *want* to know, but anyhow, they had the mattress on the back of a pickup with one of them's older brother driving, and the rest of them, including Carl, are piled in this car that's following behind. And all at once the mattress breaks loose, slides off the back of the truck onto the highway, and their car rides right up onto the mattress, and then somehow, I don't know—"

"Loses traction," Carl filled in, reappearing in the doorway. This time, he was carrying a plate. "Slides on down the road on top of the mattress a ways and then Iggy, he's the one driving our car, Iggy guns the gas and the car just, *bam!*, kicks forward and leaves the mattress behind in this kind of burst of speed. You should've been there, Uncle Micah!"

"No, he should *not* have been there, and neither should you," Liz said. "Why you're even alive to tell the tale—"

"But what does that have to do with his cast?" Micah asked.

Carl said, "Well, so many of us were in the backseat that we didn't each have our own seatbelt, see—"

"I don't want to hear!" Liz said. "I don't want to think

about it! I don't want this mentioned in my presence ever, ever again!" And she flounced off to the kitchen with her casserole.

"Okay, Mom. Jeez," Carl said. He rolled his eyes at Micah and followed her with his plate.

"Anyhow!" Suze said brightly. She was the only sister not bustling about now. She stayed in her seat and sent a flashy, social smile down the length of the table to Lily. "I don't know what you must think of us, Lily, with all our crazy family stories."

Oh, right: Lily. She seemed to have been forgotten. But she smiled back gamely and said, "I don't mind." Becoming the center of attention, however briefly, was turning her face a deep pink. "I'm just worried I won't recall every one of you-all's names later on," she said.

"It does take some doing," Dave agreed. "Especially sorting the sisters out. I'll tell you the trick, though: hair color. Ada, bottle-red. Liz and Norma, bottle-blond, and Norma is the, um, not-thin one. Suze here—" and he sent his wife a grin—"Suze is *au naturel*," he said. "Natural" was the way he pronounced it.

"I just can't be *bothered* coloring," Suze explained to Lily. "Once you start, you have to keep on. Why spend my life in the beauty parlor? To say nothing of the money."

"Oh, I know what you mean," Lily said, nodding vigorously.

Not that she herself would ever need to color. Her own hair reminded Micah of excelsior.

"And Micah, of course, is the brother . . ." Dave continued doggedly.

"Oh, *Micah* I can remember," Lily said.

This made everyone laugh. "Looky there," Phil told Micah, "you're a legend in your own time."

"What can I say?" Micah asked. "I just stand out in a crowd, I guess."

"You'll have to cut Micah some slack," Phil said to Lily. "He's the baby of the family. Me and Ada were already engaged when he was born, and even Suze was in middle school, so of course he tries to act all elderly to make up for it. All old and antisocial and crotchety."

"Oh, he's a lot more social than *my* brother," Lily said.

"You have a brother?" Suze asked her.

"Yes, Raymond; he's two years older than me. He's got his own business, this portable-commode business called Traveling Toilets, and it's all he thinks about. No girlfriend, no guy friends . . . though he does make a good living."

"Well, isn't that nice," Suze said, but in a trailing-off tone that meant she was hardly listening. Like most families, the Mortimers believed that their family was more fascinating than anybody else's. In a way, even Micah believed it, although he pretended not to.

"Ta-da!" Ada said. She was standing in the kitchen doorway, holding a giant platter of something buried in whipped cream. The twins came behind her with dessert plates, and the teenagers and young children started swarming in from the living room.

"Phil, take a photo," Ada ordered, because she prided herself on her desserts. "Has everybody kept their forks?"

No one had, apparently. Norma was sent back to fetch a new supply.

"Also," Lily was telling Suze, "Raymond would never think to clean his kitchen, I have to say."

Suze seemed confused for a moment. (As a rule, conversations in this family didn't so much flow as spray up in bursts here and there, like geysers, and she wasn't used to this pursuit of a single subject.) Finally she said, "Oh, yes. Your brother."

"Raymond doesn't even know how to do his laundry," Lily said. "He brings all his clothes to our mom to wash."

"While Micah, on the other hand, does *his* laundry every Monday morning at eight twenty-five," Dave said.

This was not remotely true, but Micah let it pass, merely lifting a palm in resignation when the others chuckled. "You would be the same way," he told Dave, "if you'd been reared in a household where the cat slept in the roasting pan."

"In the roasting pan!" Dave marveled, although he had known the family from the days when Micah's parents were alive and he should not have been surprised.

"And there wasn't a china cupboard or a food cupboard but just cupboards, period," Micah told Lily, "everything jammed in wherever it could fit or else left out on the counter. And supper might be at five p.m. or eight or not at all. And the dirty dishes piled up in the sink till there weren't any clean ones left; you had to run a used bowl under the faucet when you wanted your morning cornflakes."

"Micah had *such* a hard childhood," Norma murmured.

"I'm not saying I had a hard childhood," Micah said. "My childhood was fine. Mom and Dad were great. I'm just saying, when you grow up in that kind of chaos you vow to do things differently once you're on your own."

"Then how about me?" Ada asked him.

"You?"

She was spooning out clumps of dessert and plopping them on the plates. She paused to lick whipped cream off her thumb before she said, "I grew up in chaos too, didn't I? Suze and the twins grew up in chaos. None of *us* are fussbudgets."

"No indeedy," Micah said. (The petals of the dead chrysanthemums were scattered across the sideboard. A comic book—soaking wet, for some reason—lay on the floor near the kitchen doorway.)

"Some kids are raised in a mess," Ada said, "and they say, 'When I'm on my own, I'll be neater than God.' Others are raised in a mess and they say, 'Life is a mess, looks like, and that's just the way it is.' It's got nothing to do with their upbringing."

"It's genes," Liz said. "You remember how Grandpa Mortimer was."

"*Oh*, yes," Norma said shaking her head.

"Micah never knew him," Liz told Lily, "but he got his genes anyhow. He was the only one of us who did. Everything was just so at Grandpa's! Everything in its place! His sock drawer looked like a box of bonbons, each pair rolled and standing on end according to his instructions. Newspaper read in the proper sequence, first section first and second section next, folded back knife-sharp when he was done. Lord forbid someone should fiddle with the paper before him! He was a sign painter by profession, and all of his paints and his India inks were lined up by color in alphabetical order. The *B*s I remember especially, because there were so many of them. Beige, black, blue, brown . . . I forget what came next."

"Burgundy, maybe?" Norma suggested.

"What's so strange about that?" Micah asked. "How else would you do it?"

"*I* would trust my own common sense," Liz said. "I'd say, 'Blue, hmm—where's my blue? I remember I used it last when I did that For Rent sign yesterday.'"

Micah could just imagine what Liz's workbench would look like—the random cans and bottles intermingled with paint-stiffened brushes, old coffee mugs, a cable bill and a dog leash and a half-eaten bagel.

"The point I'm trying to make," Ada said, "is it's not so much about whether a person is messy or neat. It's whether they're accepting or they're not accepting of the way things happen to be. What we accepting ones know to say is, 'It is what it is, in the end.'"

"Well, I call that pretty discouraging," Micah said. "What's the point of living if you don't try to do things better?"

Ada shrugged and handed a child a plate of dessert. "You got me there," she said.

It was the custom for the men to clean up after family dinners. Micah was in charge of loading the dishwasher, because he had a system. Phil scraped down the grill, and Dave and Grant brought in the last of the things from the dining room. Kegger merely hung about getting underfoot. In theory, the sons and the sons-in-law were supposed to pitch in too, but this caused such a traffic jam that they soon wandered out to the backyard, where a Wiffle-ball game was in progress.

Even after the men had finished, though, the kitchen

failed to reach what Micah considered a satisfactory state. The counters were still strewn with Lego blocks and Magic Markers and pocketbooks, and for some reason the oven door refused to close.

Well, okay: he would just try to be accepting.

In the living room he found the women sprawled about in exhausted attitudes, watching a few toddlers build a racetrack on the rug. A daughter-in-law lay asleep in the recliner, but the baby in her lap was wide awake, chewing a rubber pretzel she was clutching in both hands. Micah tried twiddling his fingers at her enticingly. The baby sent him a severe look and went on chewing.

"Have a seat," Ada told him. "Move over and make room for him, Liz."

"Nah, I should be going," Micah said.

"What's your hurry? It's early yet. What do you have to get back to?"

"Oh!" Liz said, and just like that, all the other women sat up and grew alert. "Oh, what *do* you have to get back to? Nothing! An empty apartment! I *hate* that Cass has broken up with you!"

"Well, you know how it goes," Micah said.

Suze said, "Can't you reason with her? Ask her to reconsider? There must be something you could say to make her change her mind."

"Yeah, yeah, I'll think about it . . ." Micah said vaguely. "Well, thanks, Ada. Terrific meal. Tell Lily I enjoyed meeting her. And Liz, have Kegger give me a buzz when he's ready to check out computers."

Meanwhile he was making his way to the foyer, taking care not to step on racetrack pieces or toddlers. "Would it help if *I* phoned Cass?" Suze called after him, and Norma said, "You don't want to end up a crusty old bachelor!"

He made it out the front door into a crisp, smoky-smelling twilight where the only sounds were distant ones. He threw his shoulders back and drew in a long, deep breath.

He liked his family a lot, but they made him crazy sometimes.

In the car on the way home, he heard the *ding* of a text coming in. He didn't check his phone while he was driving, of course. He continued east for a few more blocks, took a left . . . and then gradually slowed down until he was barely traveling.

It wouldn't be a family member, surely. And it wouldn't be a client, not at this hour.

As soon as he saw a space, he drew over and parked at the curb. Not until then did he take his phone from his pocket. ("Good *boy*," Traffic God remarked.) He slipped his glasses up onto his forehead to peer at the screen, but the text was only from his wireless carrier, confirming receipt of his monthly payment.

It really should be against the law to send business texts in the evening.

He sat a moment longer in a kind of slump, and then he put his phone away and lowered his glasses and pulled out into the street again.

Back in his apartment (his *empty* apartment, as Liz had so helpfully pointed out), he moved about switching on lights in the kitchen and the living area and his office. He sat down in his office to check his email, but all he found was another confirmation of his monthly payment, just in case the text hadn't been sufficient.

He slid his chair away and prepared to stand, but then he paused.

All day he had felt a kind of nagging ache in the hollow of his chest. He felt as if he'd flubbed up in some way. In fact, in many ways. Getting dumped by Cass, sending Brink off who-knows-where . . . and Micah's sisters were right; it was cruel to let Lorna go on wondering whether Brink was lying dead someplace.

He slid his chair forward again and went online.

Finding her turned out to be surprisingly easy. First, he located the DC Legal Aid Society. Then he clicked on Staff, which yielded a list of lawyers. There wasn't a Lorna Bartell, but he did find a Lorna B. Adams. A click on the name, and there she was: a dark-haired woman, head and shoulders, in horn-rimmed glasses (glasses!) and a crisp white-collared blouse. He recognized her only because he was looking for her. He wouldn't have made the connection if he'd merely passed her on the sidewalk. A paragraph next to her photo stated her area of expertise—family law—and previous work experience and education. And then a phone number, a fax number, and an email address.

He chose the email address. Guessing that his message might be read first by a secretary, he kept it brief and businesslike. *Hi, Lorna, it's Micah from your college days. Thought you'd like to know I met up with Brink recently. Nice kid, seemed to be doing fine. M.* He sent it off with a whoosh and slid his chair back and stood up.

Theoretically he should feel better now, but the ache was still with him.

5

FRIDAY BEGAN with frost on the ground—unusual, for October. In fact, when Micah first stepped outside he assumed that the whitened grass was yet another trick of the eye, an early-morning clouding of his vision, and he blinked several times before he realized his mistake. The air was so cold that he could see his own breath. He would have turned back for his jacket if he hadn't known that his run would be bound to warm him up.

At this hour, the streets were deserted. By the time he got home again cars would be honking, schoolkids throng-ing the sidewalks, people waiting at the bus stop in kitchen whites and hospital blues and greens; but right now York Road was so empty that he could cross without a glance left or right, and he jogged all the way to Charles Street not meeting up with a soul.

Imagine if some cataclysm had hit the city overnight. Maybe one of those neutron bombs they used to talk about that wiped out all of humanity but left the buildings intact. How long would it take him to realize something had happened? At first he would just be glad that for once he didn't need to halt at intersections, he didn't need to swerve around a bunch of mothers pushing strollers. He would come home from his run and check his phone and feel relieved to find no messages. All the more time to take his shower, have his breakfast, see to the Friday vacuuming. But after that, *still* no messages! And no tenants banging on his door! Well, fine. He would putter a bit. Maybe start on those revisions for the update of his manual. Fix a quick sandwich for lunch but then (his phone still mysteriously silent) put together something more ambitious for supper that could stew all afternoon. Then more work on the update, but that was getting tedious now. So maybe loll on the couch with his phone awhile, playing a game of spider solitaire. Or several games, actually, because once he started playing he tended to get hooked. But so what; he had all the time in the world, it was beginning to seem.

When twilight fell he would rise from the couch and peer through one of the windows, but the azaleas blocked so much of the view that he would decide to go out front where he could see the street. No cars would be passing. No lights lit the windows across from him. No crowd waited at the lake-trout joint; no old ladies dragged their shopping carts behind them; no boys in hoodies jostled each other off the edge of the curb.

"Hello?" he would try.

Nothing.

.　　.　　.

Just before Roland Avenue he slowed to blot his face on his sleeve, and when he raised his head he saw two women in jogging suits walking side by side in front of him. "It was Chris Jennings who told me," one was saying as he drew up behind them. "I said, 'Chris, how on earth did you ever figure that out?' and Chris said, 'Oh,' he said, 'after all, I've been married twenty years, you know . . .'"

"It's just so interesting, isn't it?" the other woman said. "People can be so . . . unexpected, really."

Micah passed on by, darting a glance at their faces. He felt like a starving man staring longingly at a feast.

After that, there were suddenly swarms of people. There were men with briefcases, children with giant backpacks and cardboard dioramas and rolled-up tubes of posters. There were cars and buses and school buses, and a garbage truck with two garbage men hanging off the rear. Up by the elementary school a crossing guard stepped into the street ahead of a little boy, but then a woman got out of a station wagon some distance away and called after the boy, "No jacket?"

The boy turned and said, "Huh?"

"You forgot your jacket!" the woman called.

"Huh?"

"Your jacket," another woman told him as she walked past, and he said, "Oh," and trotted back to the station wagon.

Micah crossed with the crossing guard and then took a right, heading home.

Women kept the world running, really. (There was a definite difference between "running the world" and "keeping it running.") He dodged two teenage boys focused on one boy's cell-phone screen. Women knew all the unwritten rules: ignoring the starched and ironed linens in their hostess's powder room, they dried their hands on the hems of their slips or some ratty terry-cloth towel meant for family. Offered a bowl of fruit balanced in a precarious pyramid, they exclaimed over its elegance but declined to disarrange it. In fact Micah used to wonder, when his mother had her friends in, why she didn't just display a bowl of artificial fruit, because surely none of her guests would ever know the difference. And where did his sisters—even his harum-scarum sisters, lounging amid their household clutter—learn to make that surreptitious rubbing motion along the rims of their wineglasses when they noticed they'd left a lip-stick print? Where did the girls in his sixth-grade class learn to flip up their hair in both hands and wind it into a careless knot that somehow, without a single bobby pin, magically stayed on top of their heads except for a few bewitching tendrils corkscrewing at the napes of their necks? Watching those girls, he had thought, *I* want one. Not even a teenager yet, not even fully aware of sex, he had already longed to have a girl of his very own.

And now look. He had no one.

He slowed to a walk on the last stretch approaching York Road. He momentarily mistook the hydrant for a redhead and gave his usual shake of the shoulders at how repetitious this thought was, how repetitious *all* his thoughts were, how they ran in a deep rut and how his entire life ran in a rut, really.

He passed the lake-trout joint. FRIDAY FISH SPECIAL, the hand-lettered sign in the window read—the same sign they put out every Friday morning, so timeworn that the edges were curling. He neared the walkway to his own building and caught sight of a woman on the front stoop, sitting in the porch swing that nobody ever sat in.

His first thought was that it was Cass. This woman was not like Cass in the least; she was much smaller, and dark-haired, and the hair was cut in a pixie cap that framed her face. And her feet were set primly together, while Cass would more likely have been toeing the swing idly back and forth. But that was what happened when you were thinking of someone: every random stranger seemed to be that some-one at first glance.

"Morning," he said, climbing the steps.

"Micah?"

He recognized her by her stillness. Not by her voice—slightly hoarse, a characteristic he had forgotten—or the mountain-style twang she gave the *i* in his name, but her perfect stillness, even as she raised her gaze to him. It made her seem uncannily composed.

"Lorna," he said. He dropped his hands from his waist.

She stood up. "I came about Brink," she said.

"Right."

"Where was it you saw him?"

There was an urgency in her tone, and in the way she pressed her palms so tightly together in front of her.

"Well, here, in fact," he said.

"Here?" She looked around her. "Why would he be *here*?"

Instead of answering, he said, "You want to come inside?"

She turned immediately to retrieve her purse from the swing. He unlocked the front door—no point in avoiding the laundry room; this seemed to be an emergency—and stood aside to let her enter. She was wearing a pantsuit, navy blue and stylish, the jacket flaring out frivolously below the waist. Micah considered this unfortunate. Also unfortunate was the short haircut. It made her look . . . not serious. But she still had that intense white face, he saw when he stepped past her to lead the way down the stairs. She still had those deerlike eyes. She wasn't wearing the horn-rimmed glasses she'd been wearing in her photo.

He led her through the basement, unlocked the door to his apartment, and ushered her inside. "Sorry I haven't . . ." he began. Haven't had time to tidy up yet, he was going to say. (Several empty beer cans stood on the coffee table, along with a sheaf of junk mail and his cell phone.) But of course, what did Lorna care about how he lived? She kept her gaze fixed on his face. Two hairline cracks ran across her forehead, he was taken aback to see.

"Why on earth would he come to your place?" she asked.

"Oh, you know . . ."

This was going to be awkward.

"I gather he saw a photo of you and me in the old days," he said.

She didn't seem to comprehend.

"He was wondering about his dad, I guess, and he . . ."

Her eyes never left his face.

"I guess he thought *I* was his dad."

"*What?*"

"Well, he was just casting about, I suppose."

She felt behind her for the edge of the recliner chair and dropped into it.

"Of course I set him straight," Micah told her.

"That doesn't even . . . compute!" she said.

"I know. I told him that."

"What would put such an idea in his head?"

"Well, maybe if you told him who his dad *really* was . . ."

"Did he say anything about school?"

"School? No. He just said he went to Montague College."

"Montrose," Lorna said.

Micah sat down on the couch, first moving the rumpled afghan aside. "How did you find me?" he asked.

"Well, I got your email, of course. I always check my office mail when I wake up. And I knew you had an IT service. Marissa Baird told me. She goes to all our college reunions and picks up all the news about people."

"She would," he said wryly.

Lorna sent him a reproachful look. It was almost like the old days. "So I Googled computer repair in Baltimore," she said, "and I saw Tech Hermit. Tech Hermit was what the girls in my dorm used to call you."

"Ah, yes," he said.

"It's not like there are a whole lot of Tech Hermits in the world," she told him.

"I guess I'm pretty predictable."

She didn't disagree. "First I was going to phone you," she said. "I was halfway through dialing your number, in fact. But then I realized how early it was and I decided I should wait, and then I thought, as long I had to wait anyhow, why didn't I just come in person?"

"Oh, you could have phoned," he said. "I'm up at crack of dawn, most days."

"This was when it was still dark," she said. "I haven't been sleeping much lately." She hesitated. "And also . . . well, I always find you get straighter answers from people face-to-face."

"You thought I wouldn't give you a straight answer?"

She shrugged.

"So, he looked you up," she said, "he asked you if you were his dad . . ."

"I told him no, of course."

"And then he left?"

"Right. Well, but then later he came back. I gather he didn't have much of anything to do with himself. He ended up eating supper here. Spent the night in my guest room, ate breakfast the next morning . . . Didn't seem to have a worry in the world."

"Did he mention that his family had no notion where he was?"

"Not really, no. But I figured that out eventually on account of the texts coming in. I did say he should get in touch with you. Honest. That's kind of why he left when he did; I said he'd have to tell you his whereabouts if he wanted to stick around."

He had thought she might thank him for that, but instead she said, "He didn't give you the slightest hint where he was going next?"

Persistent little creature. She was leading with her nose, she was drilling him with her eyes.

"Not a word," he said.

"We haven't called the police yet. I'm not sure they would agree he was a missing person, even."

"No! God, no," Micah said. "He's eighteen years old."

"Yes, but—"

"And wasn't hauled off kicking and screaming, I assume."

"No . . ."

"How *did* he happen to leave?" Micah asked.

"Well, first he left school and came home, which was mystery number one. It's fall semester! He'd just started school in September! He told us he was doing fine. Not that we heard all that much from him—no more than a random text now and then. Things like *How many of those detergent-pod things do I put in the washing machine?* and *Did you pack my nose spray by any chance?* That kind of thing. But he's a teenage boy, after all. I wasn't expecting any heart-to-heart conversations."

"Well, no," Micah said.

"Then last week I came home from work and heard music playing up in his room. I climbed the stairs, knocked on his door, stuck my head in, and there he was, lying on his bed staring at the ceiling. I said, 'Brink!' I said, 'Honey? What are you doing here?' He said, 'Do I have to have a reason to be in my own room?' I said, 'But how did you get here? And what about Montrose? What about your classes?' He said, 'I hitched a ride with a guy in my dorm. I'm taking a break from my classes.' And then he turned over on his side and faced the wall."

Micah tsked.

"Well, I thought I'd give him a little time," she said. "I figured maybe he was trying to get up the nerve to tell me something. I mean, that he'd flunked out or something. But this is only October! How could he have flunked out already? At any rate, I went back downstairs, and when Roger came home I sent *him* up. Brink and Roger have this kind of . . . edgy relationship, like a lot of fathers and sons, but I thought in this case Brink might want to talk with a man. I mean, if it was some male-type thing bothering him.

But Roger got no more out of him than I had. We were both just flummoxed. So that was this last Thursday, and Brink stayed Friday, Saturday, Sunday . . . He came down for meals but he didn't talk, not even to his brother and sister. They were both thrilled to see him at first, but he wouldn't even look at them."

"Maybe he's had some kind of shock to the ego," Micah said. "Like, he'd thought he was such a big deal in high school but then he got to college and found out *everyone* was a big deal."

"Yes, I thought of that," Lorna said. "I was hoping that was all it was. So Monday I took off from work early and invited him to come grocery shopping. I was planning on the car effect. You know how kids who don't talk to their parents will spill their souls out once they get in a moving vehicle. It's like what's said in a car doesn't count. And I figured he must be going stir-crazy lying around in his room; maybe he'd be glad of any excuse to get out. Plus he and Roger had gotten into this little, like, dustup over the weekend and so I knew there was no hope *there*. Roger can act kind of heavy-handed sometimes. He just has trouble understanding that some kids need to . . . that not every kid in the world can be an instant success. So anyhow, I guess Brink decided he might as well come with me—what did he have to lose? And once we got on the road I started talking about *my* first semester in college. I said I'd felt like a country bumpkin. 'But you, now,' I told him, 'you have so much going for you, honey! Soon enough, people are going to realize that. You're so good at sports, and so musical!' Did he tell you he plays the guitar? He has perfect pitch. I don't know where he gets that from. Not from *my* side, certainly. He can summon up a phone number purely by remembering the tones it makes when you dial it."

"Really?" Micah said. This was interesting. "Wait, does a phone number sound the same on whatever kind of phone you're using?"

Lorna gave him a look.

"Sorry," he said. "You were saying?"

"We stopped for a light," Lorna went on, "and I said, 'This is why I'm thinking, Brink, that whatever little adversity you may have met up with at Montrose, you can handle it. You can get back on that horse. Because you are just a natural-born winner, I tell you.' And what did he do? He didn't say a word. Just opened his door, stepped out of the car, closed the door behind him, and walked away."

"Huh," Micah said.

"I was surprised—well, kind of hurt, really—but not all that worried. We were driving through the suburbs in broad daylight, after all; it wasn't like he couldn't make his own way home again once he'd gotten over his snit. So I bought my groceries, drove back to the house, put everything away . . . all the time expecting that he would walk in at any moment. But he didn't. That was the last I saw of him."

"Jesus," Micah said. He was trying to sound sympathetic, although frankly this didn't seem like a very alarming story. "Say," he said, "would you like coffee? I haven't had my breakfast yet."

"Oh, *I'm* sorry!" Lorna said. "Yes, coffee would be wonderful. You go ahead and fix your breakfast; don't mind me."

"Have you had breakfast yourself?"

"No, but I'm not hungry."

"You have to get some food in you. Come on out to the kitchen."

He stood up, and she rose to follow him. She said, "You know how it is when something's weighing on your heart. It feels like there's this lump in your throat and you can't imagine eating."

"Yes," he said, "I know."

He took the percolator to the sink to fill it. Lorna, meanwhile, settled on a kitchen chair. "So, he didn't mention a bit of this?" she asked him. "Leaving school, leaving home?"

"Nope. I just saw that you were texting him to find his whereabouts."

"Roger claims I should let him be," she said. "He claims Brink will run out of money soon and come on back."

"Does he *have* much money?"

"He has a debit card we set up for him to use at school," she said. "I checked his account the day after he left and he'd taken out three hundred dollars, the most that's allowed in one go. But it was from an ATM near where he got out of the car, so it didn't tell us a thing."

"Well, three hundred dollars won't last him long," Micah said.

"That's what Roger says. But Roger doesn't worry like me. Oh, he loves Brink, all right. But he's a guy, you know?"

Micah was breaking eggs into a bowl. Keeping his back to Lorna, he asked, "Have you ever thought of telling Brink who his *real* father is? I mean, his biological father?"

At first he thought she wasn't going to answer. There was a long pause. Then she said, "I don't know who his real father is."

Micah whisked the eggs with a fork.

"After you and I broke up," she said, "I sort of . . . played the field. In fact I went a little bit overboard."

Micah wondered if he'd misunderstood. She couldn't be saying what he thought she was, could she? He took a skillet from under the counter and set it on the stove, giving her time to elaborate, but when she spoke again it was only to ask, "Do you suppose he'd answer if *you* phoned him?"

"Me?"

"I mean, you two got along okay, right? It sounds as if he liked you."

"Sure, we got along fine," Micah said.

"So could you just give him a call and see if he picks up?"

Micah turned from the stove and went to the coffee table for his phone. "What's his number?" he asked.

Instead of answering, she held up her own phone, and he came closer to squint at the screen. He punched in the number and raised his phone to his ear.

It rang twice. Then Brink said, "Hello?"

His voice was clear enough so that Lorna lifted her chin sharply.

"It's Micah," Micah said.

"Oh, hey."

"So, I have your mom here," Micah said.

There was a click, and then silence.

Lorna looked stricken. "He hung up?" she asked.

"Seems so," Micah said. He stared down at his phone a moment, and then he set it on the counter.

"Why did you tell him straight out?" she asked.

"What?"

"Why did you say I was here?"

"What was I *supposed* to say?"

"Oh, just—you could have led into it more gradually. You could have asked first where he was, and how he was getting along."

"Well, excuse *me*," Micah said. "I didn't realize I was supposed to follow a script."

"Oh, I'm sorry, Micah. Forgive me," she said. (Had they had this exchange before? Somehow it felt so familiar.) Her eyes were glistening with tears, he saw. She said, "It's just that I got my hopes up, and then . . . Oh, why is he so *mad* at me?"

Micah returned to the stove. He switched a burner on and sliced a pat of butter into the skillet. "Maybe he'll call back," he said.

"You think so?"

"Maybe it was a kind of knee-jerk reaction, hanging up, and pretty soon he'll have second thoughts."

"I keep inventing reasons for why he might have left school," Lorna said. "Like, I know he had his heart set on joining this one fraternity. So if he found out they didn't want him . . . but would he have found that out so early in the school year? Well, maybe. Or if he was suspended for some kind of hazing incident. The newspapers these days are full of hazing incidents."

"Isn't it the guys already *in* the fraternities that do the hazing?" Micah asked.

"Oh. I guess you're right. Well, drinking, then. We can't kid ourselves about what goes on with the teenage drinking. Or drugs, even. At Montrose, drugs mean automatic expulsion."

"I suppose," Micah agreed. "That would explain why he didn't want to tell you the reason he left." He tipped the bowl of eggs into the skillet and started swirling them around with his fork.

"Or date rape! That's also big in the papers."

Micah turned to gape at her. "Good grief, Lorna," he said.

"What?" she said. "You don't think I'm aware that kids make bad decisions sometimes?"

"Well . . . but there are bad decisions and there are bad decisions," he told her.

She shrugged. "I've seen it all, believe me," she said.

Micah turned back to the stove and gave the eggs another swirl. He said, "You sure have changed since our college days."

"Yes," she said, "I worked at changing. I was a very narrow person back then; I realize that. I could tell it used to get on your nerves."

"You could?" he said. He hadn't known it was so apparent.

"Why, imagine how different our lives might have been if I'd just gone ahead and slept with you! No wonder it didn't work out."

"Well, that is just insulting," he said. "You really think I was so shallow?" And then, "Is *that* why you, um, played the field after we broke up?"

"I suppose," she said offhandedly. "But anyhow, what I meant about Brink was, maybe he got in some situation where he could be wrongly *accused* of date rape, is all."

Micah took two plates from the cabinet and set them on the table.

"Oh, nothing for me," she said.

"So just don't eat," he told her.

He divided the eggs with his fork and placed half on her plate, half on his. He filled two mugs with coffee and set them on the table as well.

"I wonder if our children are especially chosen for us," Lorna said in a thoughtful tone. "I wonder if the good Lord matches us up with an eye to their instructiveness."

"What could Brink instruct you in?" Micah asked.

"Well, he's just such a totally different kind of person from me."

"*That's* for sure."

She sent him a suspicious look, but he got busy fetching silverware, fetching napkins, putting out the cream and sugar.

"So, I gather you're still religious," he said when he'd settled opposite her.

"Yes, of course," she said. She hesitated. Then she said, "Or, well, I went away from it and came back to it, more like, after Brink was born."

"How about your husband?"

"How about him?"

"Is he religious?"

"Well, not so much."

"And Brink?"

"Oh, Brink's not at all a believer. Not yet. But I'm sure he'll come around eventually."

"Maybe on this little getaway!" Micah suggested in an enthusiastic tone. He was hoping to put Brink's disappearance in a more reassuring light, but Lorna just looked at him blankly.

"How'd he end up with the name Brink, anyway?" he asked.

"I named him for the youth counselor at that church I belonged to in college," she said. "Marybeth Brink. Did you ever meet Marybeth?"

"Not as I recall."

"She was the one who came to my aid when I found out I was pregnant. If not for her I don't know *what* I would have done. She saw to everything—found me a place to stay, arranged about my classwork. She's the only reason I managed to get my diploma, in the end. I was going to name the baby Marybeth if it was a little girl, but it was a boy so I named him Brink. Well, there was nary another person that I felt even halfway connected to."

Micah felt a kind of stabbing sensation. It was the word "nary" that did it—that telltale trace of country poking out of her speech like a thorn. He looked across the table at the pantsuited city lawyer and very nearly asked, "Lorna? Is that *you* in there?" What he didn't expect was how sad it made him. He no longer felt the same pull toward her; he was amazed to think that he had once spent hours wracked with lustful daydreams about her. But that was because of some change in himself. He had lost his ability to see that extra shimmer in her, so to speak.

She took a sip of coffee. "And you," she said when she'd set her mug down. "I know you and Deuce had a falling-out and you left the company."

"Yeah, the company turned out to be a really dumb idea," he said.

"So then you started Tech Hermit?"

"Well, after a while," he said.

She waited for him to say more, but he didn't. He made

his way steadily through his eggs while she sipped her coffee and watched him. Finally he felt forced to add, "First I hired on with these different IT firms here and there, but those guys were all such schmucks. So one of my customers, Mr. Girard, he got to relying on me, and when he decided to move to Florida he offered me a job looking after this building. Okay: menial as hell, and the salary was a joke, but at least it let me live rent-free with nobody bossing me around. And then gradually some of my other old customers found out where I was, and that's why I started Tech Hermit."

"I see," Lorna said.

"I guess that sounds sort of shiftless."

"No, no," she said. "I wouldn't call it shiftless. Just . . . you were being your same old self, it looks like."

"What kind of self is that?" he asked.

"Oh, you know. Not giving things a second chance."

"Come again?" he said. "I just finished telling you I've done nothing *but* give things a second chance. Made mistakes and moved on and tried all over again."

"Right," Lorna said. "And you never married?"

"Nope."

"Why not?"

Probably she imagined it had something to do with her—that her betrayal had scarred him for life or something. Which was kind of conceited, in his opinion. So he said, "Oh, I came close, a few times. But I'm not the marrying type, I guess."

"And there's nobody in your life right now?"

"Nope."

He met her gaze straight on; he refused to be embarrassed by the fact. Finally she dropped her eyes and (he was pleased to see) picked up her fork and cut into her scrambled eggs.

"How about your family?" she asked him.

"How about them?"

"Ada? Suze? The twins? Are your parents still alive?"

"No, Dad died the year I left college and then Mom a couple years later. The girls are good, though. Ada and Norma have grandchildren now."

"They were all so much fun," Lorna said. She took another forkful of eggs. "That house was like a . . . circus! When everyone got together at your folks' that time for Labor Day? Norma was teaching herself to sew and her little girls wore these dresses she'd made; remember? Brown cotton with spatulas on them because she'd used the material left over from her kitchen curtains. And Suze was nine and a half months pregnant and had to pee about ten times an hour, and whenever she got up to leave the room she'd say, 'Nature calls!' and I swear it cracked her up every time and then the whole bunch of them would fall apart laughing, mostly about *her* laughing and not about what she'd said."

"Hilarious," Micah said. His sisters did tend to have that effect on people.

"And your folks had just bought their first cordless phone and whenever it rang, everybody went into a flurry trying to find it."

"Right; one time it turned up in the laundry hamper. We never did figure *that* one out."

"And your dad had misplaced his hearing aids—"

"They were a misplacing kind of family, all right."

"—so when Norma's husband—Gregory? Gary?"

"Grant," Micah said.

"—Grant was talking about reincarnation for some reason and your dad said, all irritable, '*What's* that? Green *carnations*! What in heck are *those*?'"

This jumble of random memories felt like having his family there in the room with him—their noisiness and pell-mellness. Micah couldn't help smiling. (It was easier to smile about them when they were at one remove, so to speak.) He said, "Or at least Dad *claimed* he'd misplaced his hearing aids. Face it, he despised the things. He said all he could hear with them was the sound of his own chewing."

His cell phone rang.

Lorna froze and stared at him.

"Excuse me," he said. He stood up and went over to the counter. It wasn't a number he recognized. On the off chance that it might be Brink, he answered. "Hello?"

A man asked, "Is this Tech Hermit?"

"Yes."

"Well, my name is B. R. Monroe, and I've got the weirdest thing going on with my printer."

"I'll have to call you back," Micah said. He hung up and set the phone down again.

Lorna was still staring at him. "He's not going to call, is he," she said.

"Now, we don't know that."

"He's not," she said.

She rose to her feet and reached for her purse. "I'm going to give you my card," she said.

"You're leaving?"

"I've got to get to my office. At least I know he's alive now, and not in any danger. You'll let me know if you hear from him, won't you?"

"Sure thing," Micah said. He set her card next to his phone.

"And this time, could you just keep him with you somehow? Just get in touch with me on the sly and not let him know you did it? I can be here in no time; it would take me less than an hour."

"Only if you don't mind ending up in the morgue," Micah told her. "I'll make a deal with you: take an hour and a half and I'll keep him till you get here."

"Thank you, Micah," Lorna said.

She started toward the living area, and Micah walked past her to open the door and lead her through the basement. "Where's your car?" he asked when they had stepped out on the front stoop.

"Just over there," she told him. She gestured in the direction of the used-clothing store. Then she set a hand on his arm and stood on tiptoe to kiss his cheek. This close, he could smell the lemony scent of her shampoo or her soap or something. "It was good to see you," she said, "even under the circumstances. I appreciate all you've done."

"Oh, that's okay," he told her.

He stood back, hands jammed in his rear pockets, and watched her set off toward the street. From behind she could be any run-of-the-mill career woman, except that something about her walk seemed a little hesitant, a little lacking in briskness. It almost seemed that she wasn't quite sure where she was going. But soon enough, she turned to the right and disappeared from view.

B. R. Monroe's printer was just plain kaput, Micah found. It still responded to the Print command, but the pages it spewed forth were blank. "And now that I think back," Mr. Monroe said, "it was giving me these warning signs for the past couple of weeks or so. The printouts were getting paler and paler. I switched out all the cartridges but it didn't make the least bit of difference."

He was a middle-aged man in sweats, with a skinny gray braid down his back and a three-day growth of beard—your typical work-at-home type. His office was a disaster, empty coffee mugs everywhere and leaning stacks of pamphlets. The wrappings from the new cartridges were strewn across his desk.

"How long have you had this?" Micah asked him.

"Well, my daughter was still living at home when I bought it, I remember, because I passed my old printer on to her. And she has finished college by now and is working in New York."

Micah said, "It's got to be way out of warranty. And I can tell you right off that I'm not equipped to fix it; this is a job for the manufacturer. Even packing it up and shipping it to them would cost you more than it's worth. You're better off buying a new one."

"Shoot," Mr. Monroe said.

"Printers are cheap nowadays. You'll be surprised."

"Do I still owe you for coming out?" Mr. Monroe asked.

"Well, sure."

"You didn't *do* anything, though."

"I still have to charge you the minimum. I told you that on the phone."

Mr. Monroe sighed and padded off to get his checkbook, the soles of his rubber flip-flops smacking his bare heels.

On his way home, Micah stopped at an ATM to deposit Mr. Monroe's check. Then he picked up a few groceries at the supermarket—peanut butter and ground beef and the makings of a salad—and continued down York Road. As he turned onto his own street, he glanced reflexively toward the front stoop of his building. But no one was there, of course.

He took a right at the alley, parked in the parking lot, retrieved his groceries from the trunk, and descended the steps to his back door.

He had cleaned up from breakfast before he left on his call, but the kitchen still smelled of eggs and coffee. Lorna's chair was neatly pushed in opposite his own chair, and the table was blank and gleaming. The place gave off a kind of hollow sound, it seemed to him.

Nobody said, "You're home!" Or "Welcome back!"

He unpacked his groceries and put the peanut butter in the cabinet, the ground beef in the fridge. The salad makings he set on the counter, because it was time for lunch. But instead of starting work on that, he turned and wandered off to the living area. He still had not straightened things there. He stared bleakly at the crumpled afghan and the clutter on the coffee table—the beer cans and the junk mail. Under the surface, he thought, maybe he was more like his family than he cared to admit. Maybe he was one skipped vacuuming day away from total chaos.

He had a sudden vision of himself as he'd been the previous evening, slumped on the couch drinking too many beers and playing too many games of spider.

He left the living room and drifted into the bedroom. His bed was made up neatly, because he always saw to that as soon as he'd put on his running clothes. But the running clothes themselves were heaped on the ladderback chair, and his left top bureau drawer hung half open and his sneakers lay askew on the rug. He crossed to the bureau and closed the drawer. Then he opened the drawer next to it and studied its contents: a folded white nightgown, a hairbrush, two pairs of cotton underpants, and an olive-green sweater. Cass's store of supplies that she kept here for when she slept over.

The sweater matched her eyes exactly, but when he'd once pointed that out she had said it was the other way around; her eyes matched the sweater. "Whatever color I wear, my eyes just go along with it," she'd told him, and then, nudging him playfully in the ribs, "You should see me when I wear red!" Remembering that now, he smiled. He had liked how she never took her own good looks too seriously.

It was true that he had come close to marrying a few times. He hadn't *always* thought marriage was messy. But each new girlfriend had been a kind of negative learning experience. Zara, for instance: only in hindsight did he see what a mismatch Zara had been. She was so sharp-edged, both literally and figuratively—a shrill, vivacious mosquito of a girl, all elbows and darting movements, and it was a wonder she'd given a glance at a stick-in-the-mud like Micah. But they had hung on for nearly two years, sharing a rambling apartment next to his old campus. Then one day he picked up their phone and hit Redial, planning to continue an argument he'd started with Deuce the night before. It wasn't Deuce who answered, though, but Charlie Atwick, a dancer friend of Zara's whose booming bass voice Micah instantly recognized. "Is he gone?" Charlie had asked. "Can I come over now? I'm horny as hell."

Micah had hung up and stared at his own stunned face in the mirror.

The fact that it hit him so hard had come as a surprise, because he'd been half aware for some time of the general irritation he'd started feeling in Zara's presence. She was exhausting, to tell the truth. He should have been grateful to Charlie Atwick for giving him a reason to move on. But to be dropped so abruptly, so underhandedly, by two women in a row! He couldn't understand it. For months afterward he brooded and scowled, refusing his friends' offers to fix him up with somebody new. He didn't really have the patience, he told them, for all that meeting-and-getting-to-know. He didn't have the energy. Even after he met Adele, some part of him held back. Some part said, "Do I really want the . . . just, the *complications* of it all?" And when in the end she had sat him down and told him, in a sorrowful tone, that she was leaving him to go off and spend the rest of her life saving wolves, he had felt almost relieved. Free again! Free of all that fuss and bother.

As for Cass: well, by the time he met Cass he was forty years old, and she was not much younger. He'd figured they had nothing to prove; they were grown-ups, fully formed, at ease in their own separate lives. Whenever he thought about the two of them, he'd pictured them riding somewhere in the Kia, he intent on his driving while she gazed out her side window and hummed a little tune to herself.

What if he had told her, "Please don't give up on me. Please think twice about it."

Well, no.

He supposed she would disappear from his world now. Out of sight and forgotten, never to be seen again, the same as Lorna and the others.

Although he *did* chance to see Lorna once, he recalled, shortly after they broke up. He caught sight of her from a distance, hanging on to some boy's arm and laughing in a loopy, exaggerated way. Later a friend of Deuce's told him that she seemed to be "kind of flitting about these days"—that was how he had worded it—and Micah had asked, puzzled, "Flitting about?"

"Like, I see her with one guy one time, another guy another time, you know? And I could swear that once she was drunk."

"Lorna does not drink," Micah had said firmly. About the guys, he didn't even bother arguing. So she was walking someplace with one classmate and then walking with another; so what? At least she didn't seem to be keeping company with Larry Esmond, Lord forbid. That must have been a passing fancy.

He returned to the kitchen and took the colander from the cupboard. He rinsed a tomato under the faucet; he rinsed two heads of endive. "Awn-*deef*!" he said in his best French accent. "Zee awn-*deef* for zee sal-*lodd*!"

But his heart wasn't really in it.

6

"WHAT DID YOU THINK OF LILY?" Ada asked. She was calling in the middle of Micah's breakfast, as it happened. Having wakened in the night to the steady *drip-drip* of rain on the dead leaves outside his window, he'd turned off his radio alarm and allowed himself to sleep in and skip his morning run. He had to set down a strip of bacon and wipe his fingers before he picked his phone up. "I thought she was nice," he told her. "Kind of young to get married, though, it seemed to me."

"She's twenty-one," Ada said. "Older than *I* was when I married. But I know what you mean; she's a little . . . innocent, or something. And how is Joey going to support her? Granted, right now she has a job, but she was talking the other day about this dream she'd had: she was trying to fit twin babies into a single car seat, and everybody knows dreaming about a baby means you want one."

"Dreaming about a baby means you want one?"

"It's a sign from your subconscious that you're ready for the next stage of life."

"Well," Micah said after a moment, "you've been telling me for years that you wish Joey would act his age. Maybe this is the nudge he's been waiting for."

"Maybe," Ada said dubiously. Then, "Reverend Lowry's officiating, did I mention? Our pastor at Pillar Baptist. Lily's people don't have a church, and he said he'd be happy to do it. He came by the house last night to talk about the vows." She laughed. "He asks Joey, 'Do you love her?' And Joey thinks awhile and then he says, 'Well, sometimes.'"

"Sometimes!" Micah said.

"Oh," Ada said breezily, "all in all, I guess that's about the most a couple can hope for. By the way, I don't suppose you need an assistant tech guy, do you?"

"I barely need *myself*," Micah said. "Who did you have in mind?"

"Well, Joey, I was thinking."

This didn't even deserve an answer, in Micah's opinion. "Speaking of which, I should get busy," he told her, and she said, "Oh, okay; didn't mean to keep you."

He hung up and took another chomp of bacon.

At ten thirty he went out front to greet the carpenter—a man named Henry Bell who specialized in sealing off entry points for rodents. He was a lanky, red-bearded guy about Micah's age who'd been called in several times before (the mice around these parts were endlessly inventive), and he gave Micah a shy grin and asked, "How you doing, friend?"

"Doing good," Micah said, ushering him in.

The rain had temporarily stopped, but Henry scuffed his work boots on the mat just inside the front door. "Don't tell me those rascals found another way into your furnace room," he said.

"No, that's okay still, near as I can tell. Right now it's apartment 1B. Tenant claims they're in the kitchen."

"Exterminator been by?"

"He has. He said to tell you he saw some droppings behind the fridge."

Henry followed him through the foyer, his tool kit clanking as he walked, and Micah pressed Yolanda's doorbell.

She answered in her bathrobe, or whatever you would call it—a floor-length flowered garment with a long zipper down the front. "Morning!" she said to Henry. "You're the mouseproofer!"

"I am indeed," Henry said.

"I didn't expect you to be so tall!"

Henry turned to Micah and sent him a deadpan gaze.

"He wants to check behind your fridge," Micah told Yolanda. "That's where Pest Central suggested."

"Cookstove too," Henry said. "Is your cookstove gas or electric?" he asked Yolanda.

"Well, gas, actually," she said. She tucked a frond of hair behind her ear.

"So, they could be getting in where the gas pipe comes through the wall," he said, and he started for the kitchen with the other two trailing after him.

In the kitchen doorway, he set down his tool kit and bent over it to draw forth a long, heavy flashlight. Micah and Yolanda, blocked from entering, stayed in the hall and watched as he began making his way around the perimeter of the room, periodically tapping the flashlight against the baseboards.

"Last night I was watching TV and a mouse ran right in front of me," Yolanda said. "I'm not the scream-and-jump-on-a-chair type but I was pretty startled, let me tell you. There's something about when you see something move and you weren't expecting it, you know? Move in the very corner of your eye. You think, Eek! and your heart speeds up and the back of your neck gets prickly."

"It's atavistic," Henry tossed over his shoulder.

"Pardon?"

"It's a reflex from our caveman days."

Yolanda looked at Micah.

Henry finished his circuit of the kitchen and returned to the doorway. Both of them stood aside to let him exit and proceed back up the hall, flashlight swinging from one hand.

"Is he married, do you happen to know?" Yolanda asked Micah in a low voice.

"I have no idea."

"Hmm," she said.

She gazed after Henry thoughtfully.

"Yolanda," Micah said, "can I ask a personal question?"

She brightened and turned back to him. "Finally!" she said. "I thought it would never happen!"

"All your Internet dating and such. Going out with all those strangers. Do you ever think of giving it up? I mean, don't you ever get tired? Why do you keep on trying?"

She didn't take offense, although she easily could have. "I'm just a slow learner, I guess," she said, and she gave a little laugh. Then she sobered and said, "I think I do it for the pre stage."

"The . . ."

"The stage where I'm planning what to wear and putting on my makeup, thinking this time things might work out. And when they don't, I'm like, Well, at least *that* part was fun. That part was worth *something*. You have to pick yourself up and carry on, is what I say."

"Well, but whatever happened to learning from experience? Whatever happened to not getting into the selfsame position all over again?"

"Give up and play dead, is what you mean," she told him.

He could see that neither one of them was going to change the other's mind.

Henry had finished his inspection, evidently. He came back down the hall and bent to return his flashlight to his tool kit. "Your entry point does look to be behind your cookstove," he said, straightening. "I'm going to nail some metal sheeting around the . . . By the way, I see where your exterminator set his traps with peanut butter."

"Is that not all right?" Yolanda asked, looking up raptly into his face.

"Well, myself, I prefer tahini."

"Tahini!"

"And on top, a little sprinkle of sesame seeds."

"Sesame seeds! I thought tahini *was* sesame seeds."

"I'm just offering my personal opinion."

"Oh, right, and it makes perfect sense!" Yolanda said, practically singing.

Henry gave her a bland look. "No complaints from your other tenants?" he asked Micah.

"Not so far," Micah said. "Of course there *will* be, the minute you've finished here and gone."

Henry nodded philosophically.

"Okay, I'll leave you to it," Micah told him. "Bill comes to me, as usual."

"Sure thing," Henry said, and he bent over his tool kit again and lifted the top tray to peer beneath it.

Micah had to see himself out of the apartment. Yolanda barely noticed he was leaving.

For lunch he cut up the remains of a rotisserie chicken and tossed it with chopped celery and mayonnaise and capers. (He liked to clean out his refrigerator at some point every weekend.) As he was adding the capers he thought of a story Cass had once told him about bringing a tuna salad with capers in it to the fourth grade's opening-day picnic. "Miss," one little boy had said, "I really do like these here caprices." Quoting him to Micah, Cass's voice had become a little boy's voice, smaller than her own and livelier. Micah had always thought it sounded silly when people switched to other people's voices. In fact, he found it silly to this day, but even so he wished now that he could relive that particular moment. This time, he would just let himself enjoy the way her nose wrinkled when she talked about something that tickled her. And the triangular shape that her eyes took on; it had to do with how her cheeks rose up when she was laughing.

Caprices! Excellent word.

Halfway through eating his lunch, he got a customer call. "Tech Hermit," he said, and a woman said, "Hi!" All perkiness and optimism; she was probably still in her twenties.

"Hi," he said.

"My name is Rosalie Hayes," she said. "Is this the Hermit himself?"

"It is."

"Well, I've got the weirdest problem here. I'm living in my granny's house, right?"

"Okay . . ."

"I mean, it's my house now, because she willed it to me, but I've just recently moved in. She died of a stroke in September."

"Sorry to hear it," Micah said. He served himself another spoonful of chicken salad.

"So, she was all equipped here, technologically speaking. Computer, printer, cell phone . . . even an iPod! Actual iPod Classic."

"Lucky you," Micah said.

"But no passwords."

"No passwords?"

"I mean, I don't know her passwords. I was hoping she had a cheat sheet, but I can't find one. Just the password for her Internet, on a Post-it under her modem. No sign whatsoever of her computer password, though. And this is a *good* computer, practically brand-new. I could seriously use it. I did try calling the manufacturer, but they said they couldn't help me."

"Well, no," Micah said.

"So I was wondering if you would come to the house and see what you could do."

"Me!"

"You must know *some* special trick."

"'Fraid not," Micah told her.

"Nothing? You can't do anything?"

"Nope."

"Well, darn."

"What's her Internet password?"

"What?"

"You said you found her Internet password; what is it?"

"Well, Mildred63," she said. "Mildred was her first name, and '63 I think was the year she married Gramps."

"Try that on the computer," he said.

"I already did," she said. "And then every possible variation of it. Nothing worked. But see there? You *do* know some tricks!"

"No more than you do," he said. "You're the one who already tried it."

"The iPod's not password-protected," she said. An alluring note crept into her voice, as if she were holding out some promise. "I can work the iPod just fine!"

"Well, good."

"But I can't change any of the songs on it because they're linked to her computer. And her songs are all easy listening."

"Oh, God," he said.

"I know; right? Elevator music. Dentist music."

"My heart goes out to you," he said.

"So couldn't you just come to the house and see what you can do? I realize you must have a base fee. I understand I'd have to pay even if you can't figure out her passwords."

"I promise you I cannot figure out her passwords," he said. Then he said, "How about her mouse pad?"

"Huh?"

"A Post-it stuck under her mouse pad."

"I tried that," she said.

"Under her printer? Under a desk drawer? Under the paper in her paper tray?"

"I tried all of those."

"So then she must have used a password app. In which case, you're out of luck."

"But at least she would need a computer password to get into the password app," Rosalie said. "Am I right?"

"Not if she trusted her memory for that."

"Are you kidding? She was ancient. She wrote the street address on the back of her hand whenever she had to drive anyplace."

"Oh," Micah said.

"*Now* will you come? Please? What's your base fee?" she asked, using that wheedling tone again.

"Eighty bucks," he said.

"Eighty," she said. "I can swing it."

"Eighty bucks just to set foot in your house, with no guarantee of success. In fact, practically guaranteed failure."

"It's not an issue," she assured him. "I'm a loan officer."

"You're a loan officer?"

"At First Unified Bank. I have vast supplies of wealth at my disposal."

"You do, do you."

"If necessary, I can embezzle."

This made him laugh, finally. He said, "How far away do you live?"

"I'm in Guilford."

"Well," he said. Then, "Don't say I didn't warn you."

"I know, I know! Consider me warned. You will fail miserably, and I will contain my disappointment and hand over eighty bucks in cold cash."

He laughed again and said, "Okay, then. Your decision."

She lived in a brick center-hall colonial with maroon velvet drapes in the downstairs windows, a typical old-person house, but she herself was a slim young blonde in jeans and a wool turtleneck. A ponytail sprouted vertically from the very top of her head, reminding Micah of a pineapple spike, and her lips curved naturally upward at the corners as if she'd been born smiling. "Hermit!" she greeted him merrily.

"Micah Mortimer," he said.

"Hey, Micah; I'm Rosalie. Let me show you where the beast is."

He shucked off his rubber parka—the rain was still coming down—and folded it dry-side-out before he followed her through the hall. Persian carpet, flocked maroon wallpaper, stately grandfather clock tick-pause-ticking. They climbed the wide staircase, which was laid with another Persian carpet anchored by clinking brass rods. At the landing, they turned left and passed through what seemed to be the master bedroom. Just beyond that, at one end of a glassed-in sunporch, a gigantic desktop computer stood on a massive desk. "She *was* well-equipped," Micah murmured.

"Nothing but the best for Granny," Rosalie said.

She walked over to the computer, no doubt expecting him to follow, but instead he turned toward a smaller desk at the other end of the sunporch. This was a more ladylike affair, with a leather-framed green blotter and many tiny drawers. He set his parka and his carry-all on the seat of the chair and then lifted the blotter, exposing a few bits of paper underneath. "I know," Rosalie said, joining him. "Looks promising, doesn't it? But it's all just business cards, people's phone numbers . . ." She picked up a pale-green receipt and studied it. "I suppose at some point I should collect her dry cleaning," she said.

"Did you have any idea you were going to inherit all this?" Micah asked her.

"Not a clue. It's true I was her only grandchild, but I just assumed she'd will everything to my dad. Instead it's 'Here you go, Rosalie: house and all the furniture and forty pounds of silverware. Pots and pans in the kitchen, china in the buffet.' And I had been living in this dinky rented apartment! All I had was thrift-shop stuff! Now I own an electric fondue maker with color-coded forks."

"It's like a neutron bomb," Micah said, mostly to himself.

"A what?"

"Like when they bomb all the humans to smithereens but leave the buildings standing. I think about that, sometimes. How you'd walk into a house and say, 'Oh, look, somebody's left their professional-grade sound system. Their vinyl record collection. Their, I don't know, plasma-screen TV or something.' And you feel sort of pleased, but then gradually you realize there is no one but you to enjoy it. You're all, all alone and it's not so great after all."

"Well, I'd hardly say I'm alone," Rosalie told him. "There are at least a dozen old ladies around here bringing me baked goods."

Micah was shifting his belongings to the floor. He sat down in the chair and opened one of the desk drawers. Belatedly, he thought to ask, "Okay if I take a look?"

"Be my guest," she said, waving a hand.

In the drawer were postage stamps, a stapler, and a cellophane packet of rubber bands. He closed that drawer and opened another.

"I was thinking you could maybe just check the computer's innards or something," Rosalie said. "Press some secret button or turn some secret gear wheel."

"I did warn you," Micah reminded her. He was flipping through an appointment book—the kind that came from an art museum, with a painting on each left-hand page and a month's worth of squares on the right. All of the squares were empty.

"I just find it hard to believe that computer companies could have such faith in the average layman," Rosalie said. "Don't they know that people forget things? Lose things? Fail to write things down? How can they say, 'Okay, folks, here's a thousand-dollar computer that'll be completely and totally worthless if you happen to mislay your password'?"

"*Five*-thousand-dollar computer is more like it," Micah said absently. He was sorting through a half-empty box of Christmas cards, the Currier & Ives type. He lifted out several cards and then a miniature spiral notebook with a snowman in a stovepipe hat and "Christmas Cards Sent & Received" in lacy gold script on the cover. Tiny alphabet tabs ran down the right-hand side. He opened to a random tab. "'George and Laura Internet,'" he read aloud. "'Mildred63.'"

"Oh! Oh!" Rosalie said.

He turned to the *C* tab. "'Judy Computer, 1963mch.'"

"You're a genius!"

He handed her the notebook. "Just a little something they taught us in tech-guy school," he said.

"Really?"

"I'm kidding." He bent to open his carry-all and take out his invoice pad.

Rosalie was flipping through pages. "'Dan and Jean Wall Safe,'" she read out. "'Left 3 times to 44, right 2 times to . . .' I didn't even know she *had* a wall safe! I wonder where it is."

"You'll be finding stuff for months, I bet," Micah said as he wrote out her bill. "Christmas every day."

"Oh, Micah, I am so, so grateful to you. I can't believe you did it!"

He tore off her copy of the bill and handed it to her. Then he zipped his carryall and stood up. "Well," he said, "enjoy Judy Computer."

"Oh, I plan to!" Rosalie said. She followed him out of the sunporch and through the bedroom. It was clearly not a young person's bedroom. The bed itself was a four-poster, covered with an off-white spread made of lace or crochet work or something, and the dim oil painting above it showed a child kneeling in prayer.

"So, theoretically," Micah said, pausing to glance around, "you'll never need to buy another thing except for groceries. You've even got a whole new set of clothes. If you're feeling cold, you just hunt through the bureau and find yourself a sweater."

"Well, theoretically, yes," Rosalie said, and then she laughed and turned to open one of the bureau's drawers. She pulled out a gigantic bra—a grayish-pink contraption with mammoth circle-stitched cups, more like a piece of armor than an article of clothing. She held it up in front of her by its two straps. Even in her bulky turtleneck, she seemed absurdly small by comparison. "Ta-da!" she said, and she performed an elflike little dance across the carpet. Micah had to smile.

Downstairs in the front hall, she ducked into the coat closet and emerged with a purse. "How about the purse?" he asked when he'd tucked away the bills she handed him.

"How about it?"

"Is it yours, or is it your grandma's?"

"Oh," she said, "it's mine."

Which he'd already guessed, of course. It was small and sleek, made of brightly colored patches of vinyl stitched together.

"You know where I live now," she told him as they stepped out on the stoop.

He glanced toward the house number, puzzled.

"And you have me on your phone," she said, "if you ever feel like getting together."

"Oh. Sure thing," he said. "See you around."

And he shrugged himself into his parka and set off down the front walk.

The rain was the off-and-on kind where he had to keep adjusting his windshield wipers, and traffic was slow-moving. It took him twice as long to get home as it should have. When he finally arrived, he retrieved his car topper as he got out. Anyone who called from now on would just have to wait till Monday.

In the kitchen, he set the car topper and his carryall on

the floor and hung his parka on the doorknob. He opened the fridge and stared into it a moment, but then he shut it again. It was too early for a beer. Too late for another coffee. He didn't even want anything; he just *wished* he wanted something. In fact, now he wondered why he'd been so eager to get back home.

He went into the bedroom, where he dropped his wallet and keys into the bowl on the bureau. Without really planning to, he slid open the right-hand top drawer and gazed down into it. Nightgown, hairbrush . . .

He closed the drawer and thought for a moment. Then he took his phone from his pocket and tapped CASSIA SLADE on his Favorites list.

"Hello?" she said.

The questioning tone seemed a bad sign, since surely she knew who was calling. "Hey," he said tentatively.

"Well, hi!" she said.

He felt relieved. He said, "Hey," again, like an idiot.

"How've you been?" she asked him.

"I'm okay." He cleared his throat. He said, "I was thinking I might bring your things over. Things of yours in my bureau."

"Oh," she said.

"Is it not a good time?" he asked.

"No, no . . ."

"I mean, I could just mail them, if you'd rather."

"No, you can bring them."

"Okay," he said. A skipped beat. "Now?" he asked.

"Now is fine."

"Or would you rather have more notice."

"Now is *fine*," she said, and he thought he detected a note of exasperation.

"Okay," he said hastily. "So, see you in a few minutes."

"Right," she said.

He hung up and glowered at himself in the mirror above the bureau. He dragged his hand down the length of his face, stretching it out of shape. Then he retrieved his wallet and keys from the bowl and went to the kitchen for a paper bag.

Cass's street was lined with parked cars. All her neighbors must be home for the weekend, staying in out of the rain. But he found himself a space not too far down the block. He folded away his glasses and pulled up the hood of his parka, and then he took the bag from the backseat and headed toward her house, walking briskly, pursing his lips as if he were whistling a tune even though he wasn't. (You never could tell; she might be watching from her front window.)

The foyer had its usual musty smell from the vase of dried baby's breath on the side table. The creak of the stairs beneath his feet reminded him of all the times he'd descended them on tiptoe, hoping not to be waylaid by Mrs. Rao in the downstairs apartment; she liked to trap people in conversation. He reached the landing and switched the bag to his left hand so he could knock on Cass's door.

When she opened it, she was holding a watering can. She was wearing corduroys and a man's white shirt, her usual weekend outfit. It brought all these weekend images to Micah's mind—the two of them lounging on the couch among a welter of newspapers, or cooking some dish together, or watching some series on Netflix. But her expression was not very welcoming. She was just waiting to get this over with, it seemed. Micah said, "Hey." And then, since she still hadn't spoken, "Here you go!" and he thrust the bag at her.

She accepted it and said, "Thank you. You didn't have to bring them."

"Oh, I wanted to," he said. "I mean—"

"Right. You could use the drawer space." She glanced down into the bag. "I should have thought to take all of this with me when I left."

"How could you have thought of it?" he asked.

"What?"

"I mean, you didn't know when you left that you weren't coming back again, did you? Or, that is . . . *did* you know?"

"What? Of course not!"

"Because *I* thought we'd been having a perfectly nice evening," he said.

Out here on the landing, his voice had a kind of resonance. He worried Mrs. Rao could hear him, and he wished Cass would just invite him in. But she went on standing there with the bag of clothes and her watering can. "Remind me," she said. "Was this the evening when you suggested I should go live in my car?"

Micah felt his face turn hot.

"That was a joke," he told her. "A stupid one, I realize. I owe you an apology. I know you were stressed about your apartment. I shouldn't have teased you."

Saying "Sorry" never came easy to him, as Cass most cer-

tainly knew. He held his breath and waited for some soften-
ing in her expression.

It didn't happen, though. Instead, she said, "No, you were
right, Micah. I guess I *was* trying to change the rules, as you
put it. That was pretty dumb of me."

"Oh, no problem!" he told her.

Then her expression did alter. He couldn't say just how,
but he sensed some shift in the very atmosphere on the landing. She said, "Thanks again for bringing my things. Bye."

And she stepped back inside the apartment and closed
the door in his face.

For a full minute, Micah stood motionless. It took him
that long to collect himself. Then finally he turned and
started back down the stairs.

Before he let himself out of the house, he slipped her key
off his keychain and laid it on the side table. He wouldn't be
using it again.

On Northern Parkway, the curb lane was closed. Several
repair trucks were parked alongside the median strip, so
that drivers had to herringbone into the single lane still
open. Micah braked and sat waiting, staring straight ahead
through the back-and-forth of his wiper blades. The wait
was so long that when he heard a text arrive, he decided to
risk checking it. Who knew? It could be Cass. (*Come back!*
she might write. *I can't think what made me act that way*.)
Without shifting his gaze from the windshield, he took his
phone from his pocket and pressed his thumb to the Home
key. Then he darted a glance at the screen.

But it was only Rosalie. *Guess what i found in the safe 3 watches and the ugliest brooch u ever saw in ur life a peacock made of emeralds. This is FUN!*

He raised his eyes again to the windshield.

"Did you ever go shopping with your mom when you were a little kid?" he wanted to ask someone. (Ask Rosalie? Ask Cass?) "Did you ever walk with her down a crowded sidewalk, back when you were so small that really you were just walking with her shoes and the hem of her coat? And then—how did this happen?—you chanced to look up, and you were horrified to find that it *wasn't* your mom; it was some completely other woman with different-colored hair. It wasn't who you wanted it to be at *all*!"

Which was why, when finally he could inch the car forward, he put his phone back in his pocket and took his foot off the brake and never sent an answer to Rosalie.

7

B Y SUNDAY MORNING the rain had stopped, but the sky was still a grayish white and the air had a dank chill to it. Micah wore jeans instead of cutoffs on his run, and even so he didn't work up a sweat—not when he had to keep skirting puddles and slowing for patches of wet leaves. So he skipped his shower when he got home, and since it was his day off he skipped his shave as well and took his own sweet time over breakfast. After that, though, he couldn't seem to come up with any further ways to indulge himself. Watch TV? Nothing on but talk shows. Read a book? Nothing to be found that he hadn't already read. He started a game of spider but slammed his phone facedown on the couch halfway through. He went to his office to work on his manual, but even the preface seemed beyond redemption. "Okay, so you've got yourself a computer," it began. The slangy, bro-like tone struck him as artificial—downright embarrassing, in fact.

He decided to walk to the free-book place and pick out a book to read. Ordinarily he would bring along whatever earlier book he'd chosen and redonate it, but he couldn't find it now or even remember the title; that was how much time had passed since he'd last done any reading. Face it: he was a slug.

He set forth anyway, exiting through the basement and climbing the stairs to the foyer. But when he stepped out onto the front stoop, he found an ambulance parked at the curb. All of its lights were flashing, and its rear doors were flung open and two EMTs were loading a gurney on which Luella Carter lay flat, a mask of some kind covering the lower half of her face. Donnie Carter was patting one of her ankles and asking, "You okay, hon? Okay?" A little neighborhood boy was peering in through the passenger-side window at the controls on the dashboard.

Micah walked over to Donnie and asked, "What's going on?"

"She took a turn," Donnie said. He was a small, wiry man—smaller than his wife—and during the course of her illness he seemed to have dwindled further and lost all color. "I might could have drove her in myself," he said, "but I was scared she'd have some kind of fit and I'd land us both in a ditch."

"You need a lift to the hospital?"

"Naw, I can manage. Thanks, though. Appreciate the offer."

They stood back and watched the EMTs slam the rear doors shut. Luella had not said a word—probably couldn't, with the mask on—but something about the way her hands were clasped across her chest suggested she was at least conscious. "Well," Micah told Donnie, "let me know if there's anything I can do for you, hear?"

"Sure thing. Thanks again," Donnie said, and he turned to set off toward the parking lot.

The ambulance slid away from the curb, lights still flashing but no siren sounding, which Micah took to be a good omen. The little neighbor boy watched regretfully till it disappeared around the corner. And then, over by the used-clothing store, Micah saw Brink watching too.

The used-clothing store (which had no actual name and no sign, other than USED CLOTHING crayoned on a shirt cardboard in the window) always set a Reduced table out front on weekends. Brink was standing next to this table with a blue plastic grocery bag dangling from one hand. He had his eyes fixed on Micah, but he wasn't smiling or speaking.

Micah said, "Brink?"

"Hey," Brink said.

"What are you doing here?" Micah asked. He had to raise his voice a bit; some twenty feet lay between them.

Brink said, "Oh . . ." and held up the plastic bag. Some kind of fabric was crumpled inside it. "I needed a change of outfits," he said.

It was true that his white shirt had developed a dull, wrinkled look, and the collar no longer stood up so crisply in back. Even his corduroy blazer seemed the worse for wear.

"You've been wearing those clothes all week?" Micah said.

This was the least of what he wanted to know; he wasn't sure why he'd asked. But Brink treated the question seriously. "I bought myself a new shirt," he said, and he reached inside the bag and pulled out a forest-green jersey with white lettering across the front. GROWN-UP, the letters read.

"'Grown-up'?" Micah asked.

"I needed something long-sleeved."

He stuffed the jersey back into the bag. He still had not come any closer, and Micah—as devious as if Brink were some skittish stray animal—came no closer himself but shifted his gaze off to one side and asked, "Can I make you a cup of coffee?"

"Sure," Brink said.

Then he did approach, not so skittish after all, swinging his plastic bag.

Micah felt a kind of inner perking up—a sudden sense of purpose. He led the way back into the building, already calculating how to notify Lorna without Brink's catching on. And not only that: how to keep him till she got there. He gestured for Brink to go down the stairs first, in case he got the urge to turn and bolt, and he kept up a stream of talk to divert him. "That was Luella Carter in the ambulance. One of our tenants. She's got cancer."

"Oh, yeah?"

"Yeah, and I did tell her husband I'd be glad to drive him to the hospital but he said . . ."

They had passed through the utility rooms by now. Micah stepped forward to unlock his front door, and Brink took advantage of the pause to peek again inside his shopping bag. "I looked for boxer shorts, too, but I didn't see any," he told Micah.

"Right, I don't suppose . . ."

Something about the living area struck Micah as too revealing. His previous aimlessness and boredom hung in the air like a leftover cooking odor. But Brink appeared not to notice; he was shucking off his blazer. He tossed it on the nearest chair as they entered the kitchen, and he set his shopping bag on the table so that he could undo the first two buttons of his shirt and rip it off over his head. "I feel like *burning* that shirt," he told Micah. He took his new jersey from the bag and pulled it on, struggling to poke his face through the neck hole and then smoothing the sleeves down admiringly.

"You like?" he asked Micah.

"Looks good."

Micah started filling the percolator at the sink.

"Around where I've been staying, they don't sell *any* kind of clothes," Brink told him. "New or used, either one. Just booze and cigarettes, mostly. And gasoline for your car. Soda pop. Lottery tickets. Crab-flavored potato chips."

"Where is this?" Micah asked him.

"What?"

"Where have you been staying?"

"El Hamid? El Hajib? El *something*; I don't know."

"A hotel?"

"Or motel, more like. Or maybe not even that. The sign says 'European-style,' but all that means is there's only one bathroom per floor. It's way far downtown. Like, heading toward DC."

"So . . ." Micah said. He had to tiptoe, here. "So, how've you been getting around the city?"

"Oh, I take cabs."

"You take cabs."

Micah shook his head. He ladled ground coffee into the percolator basket.

"Well, it's not as if I could Uber," Brink said. "That would mean leaving a debit-card trail."

Grown-up, Micah thought. Right. He asked, "Have you looked for work?"

"Work?"

Micah plugged in the percolator and then turned to face Brink. "Listen," he said. "Here's what I'm going to do. I'm calling your mom to come get you."

"No!" Brink said.

But you couldn't miss the flash of pure relief that crossed his face.

"You don't want her to go on worrying, right?" Micah said. (Oh, he could be diplomatic, when necessary.) "This is killing her!"

"Did she say that?" Brink asked.

"She didn't have to say it. You could see it."

Brink studied him.

This close, Micah noticed the stray black whiskers on Brink's upper lip—one here, one there, the sparse, random prickles of someone too young to need a shave every day, although it would have been advisable. And there was a muddy look to the skin just below his eyes, as if he hadn't been sleeping well.

Bold as brass, Micah took his phone from his pocket and tapped Lorna's number.

She answered before he heard a ring, even, giving him the impression that she had been holding her breath for his call. "Micah?" she said.

"Hey, Lorna. I'm putting Brink on."

Without waiting to hear her reaction, he held out his phone to Brink. But Brink backed away, making rapid criss-crossing motions with both arms in front of his chest. "No," he mouthed soundlessly. "No."

Micah set the phone to his ear again. "On second thought, maybe not," he told Lorna.

"What? But he's there, right?" she asked him. "He's at your place?"

"Right."

"And he's okay?"

"Yup."

"Keep him. I'm coming," she said. And she hung up.

Micah returned his phone to his pocket. "Way to make her feel better," he told Brink.

"What did she say?" Brink asked.

"If you wanted to know what she said, you should have talked to her yourself."

"Did she ask how I was? Was she mad at me? Tell me her exact words."

Micah rolled his eyes.

"What? Was my dad with her? Could you tell?"

"All I could tell was she wants me to keep you here till she gets here."

"She's coming right now?"

"That's what she said."

"Did it sound like she was pissed?"

"I don't know, Brink, okay?" Micah said. And then, "I think mainly she's just concerned for you."

"Yeah, right," Brink said.

"You don't believe me?"

"Oh, everybody thinks she's so understanding and sympathetic," Brink said, "but she can be really, really judgy; take my word for it."

This didn't come as such a surprise to Micah. He had a sudden flashback to the time Lorna had lectured him about his beer consumption; he recalled the solicitous expression she had put on, the way she seemed to enjoy the taste of her own words as she told him, "My faith won't let me just stand by and watch you ruin your life, Micah." "My faith": he had felt a kind of jealousy every time he heard that phrase. He could see Brink's side of things, briefly. But then Brink asked, "Why is it that everyone acts so critical of me?"

"It's a mystery, all right," Micah said.

"My parents, my granddad, even my goddamn lacrosse coach!"

Micah took two mugs from their hooks. He said, "Is your lacrosse coach why you left college?"

"What? No, I'm talking about high school."

"Why did you leave college?" Micah asked, but he kept his back turned, so as not to seem too interested.

"I just felt like it, okay?"

Micah set the sugar bowl on the table.

Brink was checking his phone now. He seemed disappointed with the results. "I had to buy this rinky-dink charging cord from the Rite Aid," he told Micah, returning the phone to his pocket. "It takes, like, three times as long to charge as my normal cord does."

Micah tsked.

The percolator was going into its final fit now. As soon as it had finished, he filled the two mugs and handed one to Brink. "Thanks," Brink said. He carried it over to the table to spoon in some sugar, but he didn't sit down with it. "Okay if I watch TV?" he asked Micah.

"Be my guest," Micah said.

At least it was a way to keep him here till Lorna arrived, he figured as Brink walked off. Although, who was he fooling? The kid was desperate to be kept. GROWN-UP or not, he was not the least bit equipped to make it on his own.

The TV came on in Micah's office—first a succession of very adult voices discoursing seriously and then a sudden switch to the jaunty kind of music that accompanied cartoons. Micah began straightening the kitchen, pausing now and then to take a sip from his mug. When he was finished he went to his office, where he found Brink not on the couch, as he had expected, but standing beside the computer leafing through *First, Plug It In* while two children on TV talked about breakfast cereal. "You wrote this?" Brink asked, holding up the manual.

"Yup."

"So, do a lot of people buy it?"

"Some."

Brink closed the manual and studied the cover. "Do you know much about video games?" he asked.

"Not really."

"You don't play them, even?"

"I don't like things swarming all over the screen," Micah said. "Coming at me out of nowhere. Popping up at random. Disorganized."

"Really," Brink said in a thoughtful tone. He sounded like a doctor assessing his patient's symptoms.

"I did use to enjoy Tetris, once upon a time."

"Tetris!"

"You know: the one where you sort these bricks into—"

"I know what it *is*," Brink said. "It's just that it's so old-fashioned. It's not even what I'd call a video game."

"Well, one day your hotshot Fortnite and such will be old-fashioned too," Micah said. "Actually, one day we won't even *have* video games. We won't even have computers. They'll all have been hacked and we'll go back to snail mail and bricks-and-mortar shopping, and the world will start running at a manageable speed again."

Brink said, "That is just crazy talk."

"So you see why it's just as well I'm not your real dad," Micah told him.

"Right. Since my fake dad *loves* video games."

"He does?"

"That's a joke."

"Ah," Micah said. He was slightly surprised that Brink was capable of a joke.

He checked his watch. It was 11:20. What time had he placed that call to Lorna? Eleven o'clock? Later?

Time sure was passing slowly.

He sat on the edge of the daybed and looked toward the TV. Brink was using the remote now to cycle through channels. He paused at a car race but then moved on. A black-and-white movie from perhaps the 1940s slid by, a man and woman arguing in effortful, metallic, 1940s voices as if they were speaking from a stage. Brink clicked the TV off and sat down next to Micah. The sudden silence was a blessing.

"So, what did you two talk about?" Brink asked him.

"Pardon?"

"When Mom was here looking for me. Did you-all have a talk about the olden days?"

"Not really," Micah said.

"I was thinking you would discuss how you should maybe have stayed together."

"Never came up," Micah said mildly.

"Who was it who ditched who, anyhow—you or her?"

"I forget."

Brink slumped in his seat. "I bet it was her," he said finally. "On account of the way she put it: she thought you were the love of her life 'at the time.' Meaning she got disillusioned."

Micah didn't respond.

"Although," Brink added, "someone might also say that if a person had hurt their pride by breaking up with them, I guess."

"How about some lunch?" Micah asked him.

"Lunch?"

"Are you hungry?"

"I'm starving."

"All right! Coming right up!" Micah said, jumping to his feet. "Ahm-boo-*gare*, how about it?"

"Huh?"

"Hamburgers. C'est Frawnsh," he said. He was feeling more sprightly, now that he had a project.

He headed for the kitchen, with Brink trailing after him. He took the ground beef from the fridge. "Now, for a vegetable . . ." he muttered to himself, rooting through the crisper.

"You're not going to doll the burgers up, though, are you?" Brink asked.

"Nev-*air*," Micah assured him.

"What's French about them, then?"

"Me, is what. I like to speak French while I'm cooking."

Brink looked at him suspiciously.

"Afraid we don't have any buns," Micah told him. He had unearthed a few carrots and half a head of romaine, which he set on the counter along with the meat. "I bought the ground beef to make spaghetti, but you probably wouldn't like my secret recipe."

"What's your secret recipe?" Brink asked.

"Well, one of the ingredients is Campbell's tomato soup."

"Gross."

"*Potage à la tomate!*"

"You are *weird*," Brink said. He dropped onto a kitchen chair—the one that wasn't heaped with his clothing—and pulled his phone from his pocket to study it. Evidently he found nothing of interest. He returned it to his pocket and tipped his chair back on its rear legs. "You think she's bringing Dad with her?" he asked.

"No idea," Micah told him. He was forming the meat into patties.

"Cuz Mom is not real fond of driving. She might ask if he would drive her."

"Or maybe he'll want to come just because he's worried too," Micah said.

"I wouldn't count on it."

Micah's phone rang. Brink's chair crashed forward and he looked at Micah expectantly.

D L CARTER, Micah read on the screen. He answered it. "Hi, Donnie."

"Hi, Micah."

"How's Luella?"

"She's good. She's breathing fine now. I feel dumb for bringing her in."

"Nah, that wasn't so dumb."

"Well, I wanted to let you know, since you were standing by and all. I figured you might be wondering."

"Right," Micah said. He felt bad that he had not, in fact, been wondering. "I'm glad to hear things are okay."

"Well, I appreciate that. You're a good man, Micah."

"Aw, no. So, you take care, hear?"

"Will do," Donnie said.

Micah thought for a moment. Then he said, "Well, bye, I guess."

"Bye," Donnie said.

Micah hung up.

He should have asked if Luella would have to stay overnight, he realized.

Sometimes when he was dealing with people, he felt like he was operating one of those claw machines on a boardwalk, those shovel things where you tried to scoop up a prize but the controls were too unwieldy and you worked at too great a remove.

He dusted a skillet with hickory-smoked salt (sliding a glance toward Brink to make sure he didn't notice) and waited for it to get hot before he put the patties in. Then he started peeling carrots. The skillet was sizzling so loudly that it took him a moment to realize that Brink had said something. "Excuse me?" Micah asked him.

"I tend to like my burgers well-done."

"Duly noted," Micah said.

"I mean, in case you were wondering."

"Okay."

There was a silence. The skillet hissed and popped. Then, "I guess you must think I'm a spoiled rich kid," Brink said.

Micah glanced over at him.

"Right?" Brink asked.

"Well, kind of."

"You think I should get a job in construction, don't you."

Micah set the peeled carrots on the cutting board and reached for the knife.

"But it's not *my* fault my folks aren't on welfare."

Micah sliced the carrots into disks and slid them into a bowl. Then he said, "When your mom was expecting you, she had to ask her church to find her a place to live. She had to figure out how to finish her degree when she had a baby on the way and no husband to support her and no family standing by."

"What? How do you know that?"

"She told me. Did you not ever ask her?"

"Well, no."

"So now you're worrying the hell out of her just because your fully paid-for college is, I don't know, not letting you into your favorite fraternity or something."

"I got caught cheating," Brink said.

Micah stopped tearing romaine leaves and turned to look at him.

"I bought a term paper off the Internet and they found out about it," Brink said. "My professor had some sort of software that can recognize stuff from the Internet. Who'd have thunk it, right? So the Dean of Students told me I had to go home and confess to my parents and then the four of us would have a conference in his office. Discuss how we would 'handle this going forward,' was how he put it. If we *were* going forward, he said. Like maybe I might be kicked out. For a first offense! For one measly term paper! So I went home, but then I couldn't quite tell them. I knew how my mom would turn all sorrowful and my dad would take it personally. He'd be, like, 'How could you do this to us, son? What possible excuse could you have? The most elementary assignment,' he'd say, 'a standard freshman essay on the simplest possible topic!'"

"What was the topic?" Micah asked.

"Ralph Waldo Emerson's 'Self-Reliance.'"

Micah turned away hastily and flipped a hamburger patty.

"Every morning I'd get up and I'd think today was the day I would tell them. I figured I would tell Mom first and then she could tell my dad. But it seemed I couldn't do it, some- how, so in the end I left. I went to shack up with this friend who goes to GW now, except he turned out to be all involved in his, like, life, and so I came here because I couldn't think of anyplace else."

"When I was in third grade I forgot how to spell 'seize,'" Micah told him. "We were taking a test on the *i*-before-*e* rule, including the exceptions, but I don't know; 's-e-i-z-e' just didn't look right to me. So I sort of looked up at the clock and yawned and then just happened to turn my head a ways, and I saw how the kid next to me spelled it. Tuckie Smith: I'll never forget him."

"See?" Brink said. "Now you know why I had the idea you were my dad."

"No, wait; my point is, I bet every single one of us has done *something* like that. You think your parents didn't?"

"My mom sure never did," Brink said.

"Well, um . . ."

"And probably not my dad, either, or if he did he wouldn't admit it. 'Adamses do not cheat,' he'd say. 'You've really let us down, son.'"

"So, fine," Micah said. "You tell him, 'I know that, and also I let *myself* down, but I'll never do it again.' Then you all sit in the dean's office listening to his lecture, and after that you're done with it. Because I swear they won't expel you. Not for a first offense."

"They might give me an F for the course, though," Brink said.

"So? You flunk a course. Worse things have been known to happen."

Micah dished out one of the burgers, medium rare for himself, and returned the other to the stove.

"Listen," Brink said, "could I just live here with you?"

"Sorry, buddy."

Tossing the salad with bottled dressing, Micah waited for Brink to argue. But he didn't. He was quiet. He'd probably known before he asked what Micah's answer would be.

Lunch was finished and the dishes were washed (Brink ineptly drying) before the upstairs buzzer finally rang. By then Micah was sitting on the living-room couch with the Sunday paper, pretending to read about last night's World Series game even though he had no interest in either team, and Brink was back in the office watching what sounded like a gangster movie.

Zzzt, the buzzer went—more of a snarl than a ring, like an angry, insistent wasp. It was loud enough to be heard in the office, but no sign of stirring came from there. Micah called, "Brink?"

No sound but machine guns.

"Brink!"

Micah rose, finally, and went out to the basement and climbed the stairs to the foyer. When he opened the outside door he found not only Lorna but a thin, bearded man who was standing just behind her. "Is he here?" Lorna asked. She was looking past Micah, searchingly. "Do you still have him?"

"I do," Micah said.

She was in casual clothes today, slacks and a cable-knit sweater, and her husband wore a cardigan over his button-front shirt. He seemed milder and less big-wheelish than Micah had envisioned. His eyes sagged at the outer corners and his beard was streaked with gray. "Roger Adams," he said quietly, offering his hand to Micah, and Lorna said, "Oh! I'm sorry. Micah, meet Roger. Roger, this is Micah."

"Come on in," Micah told them. "Brink is watching TV."

He turned to lead them through the foyer and down the stairs, through the laundry room and the furnace room. One of the washing machines was in use and the air smelled damp and bleachy, but Micah was long past any concern about appearances. It was occurring to him that Brink might have seized his chance to make an escape through the rear exit. When they entered the apartment, though, they found him standing in the office doorway with the TV still blaring behind him. He was holding the remote control in one hand, as if his parents and Micah were the ones he was about to switch off, and he wore a frozen, defensive expression.

Lorna said, "Sweetheart!" and she rushed across the room to throw her arms around him. Brink gazed over her head toward his father, but with his free hand he was patting her back. "Hi, Mom," he said. "Hi, Dad."

"Son," Roger said, nodding. He remained standing next to Micah; he kept his hands in his trouser pockets.

"Are you all right?" Lorna asked Brink, drawing back. She looked up into his face. "Have you lost weight? You have! What on earth is that you're wearing?"

Brink shrugged. "I'm fine," he told her.

"How long has it been since you shaved? You're not growing a beard, are you?"

"Lorna," Roger said.

"What? I'm only asking," Lorna said. She told Brink, "We've been out of our minds about you! What have you been eating? Where have you been staying?"

"Let him get a word in, Lorna," Roger said.

"What are you *talking* about?" she asked, wheeling on him. "I'm *begging* him to get a word in!"

"Now, Lor."

"I'll just, um, turn the TV off," Micah said, and he went into the office. A woman was strolling down a beach while a man's disembodied voice rattled off a medication's side effects at breakneck speed. Lacking the remote, Micah pressed the power button and then waited a bit before heading back out to the living room. Not much had changed there. Roger's hands were still in his pockets, and Lorna had looped an arm through Brink's left arm. "First we thought you might have gone to stay with a friend," she was telling him, "but your friends are all away at college now, so we weren't—"

"Would anyone care for coffee?" Micah asked. "How about I make us a pot."

No one answered, for a moment. Then Roger said, "That would be good of you, Micah."

Micah moved toward the kitchen area, thinking this would give them some privacy, but for some reason they all came with him. Lorna was saying, "I *was* going to call some of your friends' parents, but your dad said . . ."

Micah took the percolator to the sink to fill it, and Roger drifted over to stand next to him and watch, as if he found the process fascinating.

". . . and I knew he had a point but I was just beside myself; I couldn't think what to . . ."

Micah spooned ground coffee into the percolator basket, replaced the lid, and plugged the cord into the outlet. When he turned from the counter he found Lorna still clinging to Brink, still fixing her eyes on his face as she talked. Brink had set the remote on the table and he was looking off to one side.

"Why was it you came *here*, son?" Roger asked during a pause.

Brink focused on him. At first it seemed he wasn't going to answer, but then he said, "I remembered they sold used clothing next door and I needed something to wear."

"What? I mean, why was it you came to Baltimore? Why to Micah?"

"I thought he might be my dad," Brink said.

This wasn't news to Lorna, of course, but Roger must not have been told. "Your dad!" he said.

"It sounded like we had some traits in common."

"You had traits in common with Micah," Roger repeated slowly.

Micah stiffened. He was about to take serious offense.

"With a man who earns his own living," Roger said. "Who appears to be self-sufficient. Who works very hard, I assume, and expects no handouts."

Brink was staring blankly at his father.

"Sorry, son," Roger said, "but I fail to see the resemblance."

Just like that, as if he'd planned it all along, Brink freed his arm from Lorna's and turned to open the back door and walk out. It remained ajar behind him, letting in light and cold air.

"Oh, Roger!" Lorna said. "Brink? Come back! Go after him, Roger!"

But it was she who went after him, dislodging a kitchen chair in her path and tearing out the door and click-clicking up the steps.

Roger turned and gave Micah a look. "I apologize, Micah," he said.

"That's all right," Micah said.

"I hope we didn't wreck your Sunday."

"Nah, I didn't have any plans."

Roger held out his hand; it took Micah a moment to realize that he wanted to shake again. Then he left, showing no sign of haste. He was the only one of the three who thought to close the door behind him.

Micah stood there awhile.

The percolator worked away peacefully on the counter.

He didn't know what he had expected. A touching reunion scene? A group hug in his kitchen?

He picked up the remote, planning to return it to his office, but then he noticed Brink's clothes on the chair—his dingy white shirt and his crumpled blazer. He set the remote down again and gathered the clothes in a clump and went to open the back door. "Hello?" he called up the stairwell.

No answer.

He climbed the steps and looked out over the parking lot. He saw Lorna walking toward him at a leisurely pace, her arms folded across her chest. "The two of them are having a talk," she explained once she was closer. "Roger told me to give them a minute."

"Well, Brink forgot his clothes," Micah said. He held them up, and she reached out to take them. "Come inside and I'll pour you some coffee," he told her.

"I don't want to disrupt your schedule."

It was a little late to think of that, but he didn't say so. He gestured toward the steps and stood back to let her go first. Without seeming to realize what she was doing, she lifted Brink's clothes to her nose and drew in a long, deep breath as she descended.

In the kitchen, she sat down on one of the chairs and laid Brink's clothes on the table. Micah busied himself with getting the mugs out, and two spoons and two paper napkins.

"I could just *shoot* Roger," she told him.

"Huh?"

"Finding fault that way. This is not the time to nitpick!"

"Oh, well . . ."

"I'm sorry you didn't get to see him at his best," she said. "He's really a very nice man."

"I liked him, in fact," Micah told her.

"You did?" she said. Then she said, "I got the feeling he liked *you*, too."

"You sound surprised," Micah said.

"No, no . . ." She studied him. "In a funny way, you two are not so different," she said.

"Well," he said, "except he's a corporate lawyer and I'm a

glorified handyman. Little details like that. He owns a house and I live in a basement. He has a wife and three children and I am on my own."

"But not for good, surely," she said. "I'm sure you'll find somebody."

"It's beginning to look like I won't," he said.

"Well, I'm sorry to hear it."

So far Micah had been standing at the kitchen counter, but now he crossed to the chair opposite hers and dropped into it. "Do you know why that is?" he asked her.

"No, why?"

"I meant that as a real question. Do you know what it is about me that turns women off?"

"Turns women off! You don't turn women off!"

"In the end I do," he said. "Things seem to start out great, but then . . . I can't explain what happens. They start giving me these sideways kinds of glances. They start acting kind of distracted. It's like all at once they remember somewhere else they'd prefer to be."

"I can't imagine that's really true," she told him.

"It was true of you," he said.

"Me! It wasn't me who broke up!"

"You were the one who kissed Larry Esmond," he said.

"Oh, for mercy's sakes, Micah. Not Larry Esmond again."

"One day I was the love of your life and the next day you're kissing Larry."

She clasped her hands on the table and leaned toward him, earnestly. (He could imagine, all at once, how it would feel to be one of her clients.) "Listen," she told him. "I said this before and I'll say it again: Larry was nothing to me. He was this meek young man in my Bible class; I'd barely exchanged two words with him. But that afternoon I was walking across the campus, I happened to be feeling kind of low, and I saw Larry coming toward me and when he got near he stopped short and he said, real quietlike, 'Lorna Bartell.' Like my name was important to him. He didn't smile, didn't wave, he was wearing this solemn expression and looking into my face and 'Lorna Bartell,' he said. Like he really did see me, really saw my true self. And I stopped too, and I said, 'Oh, Larry.' Because you and I were going through a rough patch just then, and I was feeling kind of miserable."

"We were going through a rough patch?" Micah asked.

"But that kiss was not intentional! Not on my part, I mean. I just wanted to tell somebody about my troubles, and he seemed glad to listen. He sat down on a bench with me and let me pour it all out. Then, I don't know, he kind of leaned close and kissed me, which came as such a surprise that I let him, for a moment. But when I told you that, you didn't believe me. You refused to see that a person might sometimes just . . . make a little misstep."

"*I* didn't know we were going through a rough patch," Micah said.

"I was miserable," she said.

"You were miserable?"

"Micah," she said, "remember the bicycle you lost in the park the summer you turned twelve?"

"Twelve! We hadn't even met when I was twelve."

"Maybe not, but you told me all about that bicycle. It had ten speeds, remember? And these elegant skinny tires instead of balloon tires."

"I remember," he said grudgingly, because the memory wasn't a happy one.

"You got it for your twelfth birthday, after you begged and pleaded. You swore you'd never ask for another thing; they could skip your Christmas gifts and next year's birthday too, you said. Then a few weeks after you got it, you rode it to the park to shoot baskets with a couple of friends. And you got caught up in your game and you played till it was dark, and then you went for your bike but it was gone."

Micah shook his head sorrowfully. "One of the tragedies of my life," he said, and he was only half joking.

"I mean, how could you have forgotten it? How could you have forgotten that bike for a whole afternoon? Wouldn't it have been on your mind every single minute, something you'd wanted for so long? But no, by then you were used to it. Now that it was yours you were noticing things wrong with it, like squeaky brakes or a scratch in the paint or, I don't know, and it didn't matter anymore."

"It wasn't that it didn't *matter*," Micah told her.

"Well," Lorna said steadily, "I am the bicycle you lost in the park the summer you turned twelve."

He blinked.

"You didn't think I was so great anymore," she said. "You started finding fault with all I said; you looked bored when I was talking; you acted like everyone else in the room was more important than I was. You had stopped properly valuing me."

"I had?" he said.

"And then when that Larry business happened, when I tried to explain how it came about, you wouldn't listen. It was almost like you were glad of the excuse. 'No,' you told me, 'that's it. We're done.' I said, 'Micah, *please* let's not break up!' but you just walked away and I never saw you again."

"Wait. You're saying that was *my* fault?" he asked.

And yet, at the same time, he was visited by a kind of translucent scarf of a memory floating down upon him. He recalled the vague dissatisfaction he'd started feeling in her presence, and his suspicion that she, in turn, had begun to notice his own flaws. It was dawning on him, he remembered now, that theirs was not the perfect love he had once imagined it to be.

"But in any case!" Lorna said, suddenly brisk. "That's all over and done with, right? You have yourself a good life, it looks like, and I truly believe you're going to find the right person by and by. And I have *my* right person, and three children who are my pride and joy, even if one of them does happen to be going through a difficult stage at the moment. But I know he'll turn out okay."

"Oh, yes," Micah said absently. He was still trying to adjust to this altered view of the past.

"Roger and he will have a nice talk, and Brink will come around. I know he will."

She sat back, then. She reached for Brink's blazer on the table and held it up in front of her, shook out the wrinkles, and folded it neatly in half. "Sometimes," she said musingly, "you can think back on your life and almost believe it was laid out for you in advance, like this plain clear path you were destined to take even if it looked like nothing but brambles and stobs at the time. You know?"

"Well . . ." Micah said.

"So, tell me!" she said. She set the blazer aside. "Do you ever hear from—"

There was a knock on the back door, then—three firm raps, clearly Roger's knock rather than Brink's. But when

Micah rose to answer he found both of them standing there, Brink alongside his father.

"Well, hey," Micah said.

Neither one of them spoke. Brink's expression was sullen, his eyes lowered, and Roger's eyes were on Brink even as he moved aside to let Micah close the door behind them.

"Welcome back!" Lorna caroled. She had risen from her place at the table, and she was clasping her hands in front of her.

Roger said, "Son?"

"I'm *getting* to it," Brink told him.

He took a step toward Lorna. He had raised his eyes by now. "Mom," he said, "I was under a lot of pressure because I'd been caught kind of like fudging on this paper that was due and the dean said I had to go home and tell my parents and then we should all have a conference about how to handle it going forward so I was feeling really stressed and that was why I left."

He came to a full stop. Eyes still on Lorna, he didn't move a muscle.

It took Lorna a moment to sort her way through to the kernel of this. Then she said, "What do you mean, 'fudging'?"

Brink cast a glance back at Roger. Roger gazed at him sternly.

"I was running out of time," Brink said finally, turning to Lorna again. "They pile too much work on us there! The paper was due the next day but so were a lot of other things too and so I . . . guess you could say I . . . bought one online."

"Oh, Brink!" Lorna cried.

Brink clamped his mouth tightly shut.

"Oh, how *could* you? How could someone so bright and talented and—"

"Lorna," Roger said warningly.

Which was lucky, because otherwise Micah might have said it for him.

Lorna stopped speaking.

Brink sent another glance toward his father. He cleared his throat. "The plan is to go back to school and face the consequences," he said, turning once more to Lorna, "and after that I'm going to get down to work and make you proud of me again."

This had such an inauthentic ring that Micah suspected Roger had dictated the words, but Lorna's face softened and she said, "Oh, honey, I'll always be proud of you! Both of us will. Won't we, Roger?"

Roger said, "Mmm-hmm."

She stepped forward to give Brink a hug, and he stood motionless within her embrace while Roger looked on benignly, hands in his trouser pockets, jingling keys or coins.

When Lorna drew back, she was suddenly all business. "Let's get you home," she told Brink. "We'll have a nice Sunday evening together, a cozy family evening, and we'll go to the Dean tomorrow. Oh, the little ones will be so glad to see you!"

She turned to collect Brink's clothes from the table, one arm still wrapped around him as if she worried he'd get away from her, and then she guided him toward the door. Roger opened it for them, but after he'd followed them out he looked back to say, "Thanks, Micah."

"Anytime," Micah said.

"Yes! Oh!" Lorna said, pivoting. "Thank you so *much*! I don't know how we can ever . . ."

Micah tilted a hand to his temple, and then he closed the door after them.

The percolator was merely sighing now. The coffee must be way overbrewed. Next to it sat the empty mugs, the spoons and napkins, everything ready for guests. Only there were no guests.

He put the spoons away in the drawer. He put the napkins back in their cellophane packet. He hung the mugs on their hooks, and then he unplugged the percolator and emptied the coffee down the drain.

8

YOU HAVE TO WONDER what goes through the mind of such a man. Such a narrow and limited man; so closed off. He has nothing to look forward to, nothing to daydream about. He wakes on a Monday morning and the light through the slit-eyed window is a bleak, hopeless gray, and the news on the clock radio is all unspeakably sad. There's been a mass shooting in a synagogue; whole families are dying in Yemen; immigrant children torn from their parents will never, ever be the same, even if by some unlikely chance they are reunited tomorrow. Micah hears all this dully. It doesn't surprise him.

He tries to slide into sleep again but it's a fitful, fretful sleep, broken by fragments of dreams. He dreams he dropped his wallet and it landed in Sofia, Bulgaria. He dreams he swallowed a wad of chewing gum, although he hasn't chewed gum since grade school.

He gives up and struggles out of bed and trudges to the bathroom, and then he gets into his running clothes and switches off his radio and exits through the basement. Climbing the stairs to the foyer, he feels the need to assist himself by pushing down on his thighs with his palms. He feels heavy.

Outside, the air smells like diesel. The ground is still damp from Saturday's rain. He starts at a slow, bumbling pace; it seems that some blockage in his chest is restricting his breathing. He crosses the street and heads north. His chest begins to loosen and he speeds up a bit. He sees people waiting at the bus stop, but when he turns west and leaves his own neighborhood the sidewalks are almost deserted. Just a couple of other runners pass on the opposite side of the street, and a workman unloads traffic cones from a truck at an intersection. Not till Roland Avenue does the school crowd begin to appear. Little ones dawdling, mothers urging them along, older children tripping each other and jostling and teasing.

Turning south, finally, on the homeward loop of his run, Micah sees an ancient, stooped man clinging to a wrought-iron railing as he inches down his front steps with his brief-case. The man crosses to an out-of-date Buick and opens the door with one crabbed hand and heaves the briefcase onto the front seat; then he shuts the door inconclusively and makes his way around the hood, both hands maintaining constant contact with the car until he reaches the driver's side and opens that door and disappears within by infini-tesimal degrees. Something tells Micah not to offer help, although he does slow to a walk until the man is safely settled.

He's fully aware that old age will be coming for him too, in time. Health troubles, insurance issues, all with no hope of a pension. Even now, in his forties, he has started to feel slightly less trustful of his own body. He takes more care about how he lifts things, and he gets winded sooner on his runs. A long-ago basketball injury tends to set up a kind of echo in his left ankle during sudden changes in the weather.

Heading east now, he comes across a huge boxwood veiled in fake cobwebs for Halloween. He veers around two women competing to feed a parking meter. Briefly, he mistakes a newspaper box for a child in a bulky jacket. He has noticed that his faulty vision most often reveals itself in attempts to convert inanimate objects into human beings.

He approaches his building from the front, slowing to a walk after he's passed the lake-trout joint. He sets both hands to his waist, breathing hard, as he climbs the steps to the stoop. He sends a reflexive glance toward the swing, but of course nobody is waiting there.

His shower is hot and invigorating, and he likes the smell of the soap he recently bought at the Giant. But once he is out again and standing at the sink, towel wrapped around his waist, it emerges that he's not up to shaving. He clears an arc in the condensation on the mirror with the heel of one hand and stares at his own face and just cannot, cannot be bothered. Since he skipped his shave yesterday, his whiskers are already noticeable—a grainy black mask dotted with random glints of white. He looks dirty.

Well, so what.

In the bedroom he gets dressed, and then he goes out to

the kitchen to make his breakfast. Toast, he decides, and an orange half that's been waiting facedown on a saucer in the fridge for the past few days. Its surface has developed a dried-out, beaded-over appearance, but never mind. He cuts it into wedges with a steak knife. He doesn't bother with coffee. He doesn't even bother sitting down; just stands at the counter, alternately chomping on his toast and sucking orange wedges. There's a calendar tacked to the wall above him but it's still turned to August. He doesn't really use paper calendars anymore. He studies August's photo: a woebegone beige puppy with a bandage covering one eye. The calendar came in the mail from an animal-rescue outfit.

Yet another dream floats into his mind from this morning: He was riding in a car with his father. He was telling his father that he absolutely refused to visit Aunt Bertha again. This dream was so vivid, so full of concrete detail, that he can still smell the car's dusty felt upholstery. However, the father in his dream was not anyone he knows, and he has never had an Aunt Bertha. It appears that he was accidentally dreaming somebody else's dream. Now that he thinks about it, his other dreams this morning may have been borrowed as well.

He tosses the remains of his toast into the garbage along with the orange peels. He rinses the saucer under the faucet and returns it to the cabinet; he rinses the steak knife and returns it to the drawer. There's no point in running the stick vacuum around the table because he hasn't sat at the table. So, straight ahead to floor-mopping day. "Zee dreaded moppink," he says aloud. But he makes no move to fetch the mop and bucket.

Instead he goes into his office and checks his email. Ads

for political candidates, pleas for political contributions, huge savings on snow tires and malware protection and gutter cleaning. Delete, delete, delete. Kegger wants to know if Wednesday they could meet at the Apple Store. Go ahead and say yes; a glimpse of family sounds like not such a bad idea right now. His subscription to *Tech Tattler* will expire at the end of next month and he should click here. Delete.

He's about to log off when he sees he's received a text from Lorna Bartell Adams. *Just wanted to tell you . . .* the top line begins. This is why he should keep his phone with him at all times; he's forever playing catch-up. He clicks on the icon to read the rest of it. *Just wanted to tell you that all is well here. We had a nice long talk on the drive home and Monday we're setting up an appointment with the dean. Thank you again. XX Lorna*

He considers answering this, but in the end he doesn't. What would he say, anyhow? *I'm surprised you even bothered writing since supposedly I am such a—*

He pushes back from his desk and rises and goes to the living room. Afghan, phone, three empty beer cans, carry-out menu, potato-chip bag. He puts everything in its rightful place. Not for the first time, it occurs to him that he really should take care of all this before he goes to bed every night. But somehow, at the end of an entire day of doing everything he was supposed to he just runs out of enthusiasm.

How come what went wrong with us ended up being MY fault? What on earth do you imagine I—

He gives his head a little shake. Move on, for Christ's sake. Lorna is over and done with. All of them are—Zara too, and Adele, and finally Cass. He ought to feel liberated. He *does* feel liberated. Lorna so tediously self-righteous, Zara so obsessed with The Dance (as she called it), Adele with her precious endangered species. ("Are you sitting down?" she would ask before announcing the demise of some rare breed of butterfly. Even though she was right there in the room with him and could see for herself that he was indeed sitting down. "Are you ready for this?" she'd ask. Like someone laughing at her own joke, instructively, before beginning to tell it.) And Cass: Well, there's a lot about Cass that he could find fault with, starting with the fact that she has been completely dishonest about what she was expecting from him. How was *he* to know what she expected? He's not a mind reader!

He frowns down into the wastebasket where he's just dropped the potato-chip bag. Then his phone rings, and he takes it from his pocket to check the screen. Unfamiliar number.

He answers. "Tech Hermit," he says.

A woman asks, "Tech Hermit?"

He rolls his eyes. "Yes," he says.

"So, I have this dilemma?" she says. Her voice is young but not *that* young. She ought to have given up on the rising inflection by now. "Sometimes something just quits on me? Like this program I'm running? And then I get this note on my screen offering to report it for me?"

"Mmm-hmm."

"Well, do I go ahead and say yes or is that just inviting trouble."

Ironically, her one actual question has no question mark at the end.

"Why would that be inviting trouble?" Micah asks.

"Because they might steal my identity?"

"Excuse me?"

"My *identity*. It might be a plot to steal it."

"Nah," he says.

"No?"

"Not a chance."

There's a silence, as if she's debating whether or not to believe him.

"You should be fine sending a report," he tells her, "but don't bother doing it if it's going to make you uncomfortable."

Anyhow, he very nearly adds, there are lots worse things than losing your identity. Right now he almost feels that losing his own identity would be a plus.

"Okay, thanks," she says finally, and she hangs up.

Doesn't ask if she owes him anything, not that he'd have said yes.

He takes the wastebasket to the kitchen and dumps it into the garbage container underneath the sink. Tomorrow is collection day, but he doesn't have enough garbage of his own to fill a single bag, even.

His next call comes some time later, while he's idly flipping through the *Sun* at the kitchen table. "It's Arthur James," a man says. "Do you remember me?"

Micah says, "Um . . ."

"You set up an external disk for me a couple of months ago."

"*Oh*, yes," Micah says—convincingly, he hopes.

"Well, all at once my printer can't scan. Yesterday it could scan but today it seems it can't."

"Did you try turning it off and then on again?"

"Yes, but nothing happened."

"Hmm."

"So I was wondering if you would come and take a look."

"Remind me what your address is?"

The man tells him, and Micah jots it down on the memo pad next to the toaster. "I'm on my way," he says. He hangs up and tears the page off the pad, grabs his car topper and his carryall, and heads out the back door.

It's late morning by now and there's a call-in talk show on the car radio. Micah thinks call-in shows are the worst idea going. Who cares about some man-on-the-street's ill-informed opinion? He keeps meaning to switch stations, but he doesn't have the energy.

The current caller, a gravel-voiced man from Iowa, sounds surprised to find himself on the air. "Hello?" he says. "Am I on?"

"Yes, yes," the moderator says impatiently.

Then the man of course has to embark on the usual introductory flourishes. "Well, hi!" he says. "Good morning!" Pause.

"Go ahead, please."

"Well, first off," the caller says, "I just want to tell you how much I enjoy your show. I always—"

"What's on your mind?" the moderator asks.

"Huh? And also I'd like to thank you for answering my—"

"You're welcome! What are you calling about?"

The caller goes into a rambling discussion of . . . what is the topic today? Police violence; something about police violence. He is full of verbal tics—"y'know" sprinkling every sentence and so many "um"s and "uh"s that you'd think he would hear them himself. But he's oblivious, even when the moderator starts giving him hurry-up nudges like "Yes, well—" and "Okay! Well—"

"This is why you should leave radio to the professionals," Micah chides the caller. Then he tackles the moderator. "And a little common civility from *you*, please."

A giant tanker truck is blocking the next intersection. Traffic God must be having fits. All in all it causes quite a delay, and by the time Micah's on the move again the call has mercifully ended and the news is airing. There are flash floods in Jordan and a catastrophic mudslide in Colombia. An illegal immigrant who's being deported to his homeland says that when he gets there he'll just turn around and come back. Try again, try again, and try again after that, he says, because what else can a person do? Micah finally cuts the radio off. He's stopped for the light at Northern Parkway now and he can hear a neighboring car's radio playing something hip-hop and feverish, the beat so heavy that it makes his eardrums thud. He waits facing straight ahead, his hands placed on the wheel at precisely ten o'clock and two o'clock. He mentally writes another text to Lorna.

The only place I went wrong, he writes, *was expecting things to be perfect.*

Abruptly, he signals for a turn, and when the light changes he heads east instead of continuing north.

Now that his radio is silent, he can hear all the sounds outside his car and inside. The hissing of the tires on the damp pavement, the sewing-machine hum of the engine, some tool in his carryall rattling against another tool with every slight jog in the pavement. He passes Loch Raven Boulevard. He passes Perring Parkway.

He takes a right on Harford Road.

It's 11:18. He has no idea what the fourth grade would be doing now. Is it lunchtime yet? He'll wait for lunchtime. He'll just park in the lot and wait. Except, how will he know that it's lunchtime? They'll be indoors, after all, in the cafeteria. Then will they come outdoors once they've eaten, or will they stay in till afternoon recess? Well, if he has to wait till afternoon, he will. He'll just sit in his car till afternoon, because what else can a person do?

He takes a right, a left, another right. He's traveling through a mostly residential section, small houses with small, leaf-littered yards, many with signs out front for home enterprises like hair weaving and knitting supplies. Then he passes a baseball diamond and he dead-ends at Linchpin Elementary. Tired-looking two-story brick building, crumble-edged concrete steps, garish paintings in most of the windows. Bare clay playground to the left with a swing set, a jungle gym . . . and yes, children, by the dozens.

At first he's encouraged. He parks on the asphalt lot and gets out of the car, still wearing his glasses because he needs to see what's what. But then it strikes him that these children look too young to be fourth-graders. They're playing a circle game, something on the order of ring-around-the-rosy, and they have the bunchy, squat, bundled appearance of children dressed by grown-ups. Even so, Micah continues walking toward them. He has spotted another group just beyond them, an older group, the boys and girls more separated. The boys are scuffling together without any clear purpose while the girls have organized some sort of jump-rope game. "Down in the valley where the green grass grows," they're chanting as the rope twirls, "there sat Allison sweet as a rose." Allison must be the girl who's jumping, her braids flying up behind her every time she lands. "Along came Andrew and kissed her on the cheek—"

"Andrew *Evans*?" Allison shrieks. "Yuck!"

"How many kisses did she get this week? One, two—"

"Fourth grade?" Micah asks the nearest rope turner.

"What?"

"Is this the fourth grade?"

"Well, some of it."

"Where's your teacher?"

"Uh . . ."

The girl looks around vaguely. She allows her end of the rope to slow, and Allison trips and comes to a halt. "No fair!" Allison cries, and she tells the others, "Shawanda let the rope die!"

"Sorry, that was my fault," Micah says. "I'm trying to find—"

He starts to circle around them, but there seems to be a tossed-off jacket on the ground where he didn't expect it. It snatches his left shoe and brings him to his knees. "I need to find your teacher," he finishes as he struggles to rise. He isn't hurt in the least, already he's on his feet again, but apparently the mishap has alarmed the little girls, because they're turning toward the building and calling, "Ms. Slade! Ms. Slade!" ("Mislaid! Mislaid!" it sounds like.) "There's a *man* here!" they call.

"I just wanted to have a word with her," Micah tells them, and then, "A word with *you*," because now Cass herself has appeared, stepping out of a side door. She has her head lowered and she's zipping her parka as she walks; she doesn't notice him till she's only a few feet away, and then she looks up and her forehead creases and she says, "Micah?"

"I've done everything wrong," he tells her. "I was trying to make no mistakes at all and look at where it got me."

"What?"

"Look at where I've ended up! My life has come to nothing! I don't know how I'm going to go on with it!"

"Oh, Micah," she says, and then she steps closer and gently takes hold of his wrists, because he seems to be wringing his hands. She looks down at his knees, caked with damp clay, and she asks, "What *happened* to you?"

"He fell over my jacket," a little girl says. She has picked the jacket up from the ground and is brushing it off efficiently.

But Micah chooses to misunderstand Cass's question. "I'm a roomful of broken hearts," he tells her.

She says, "Oh, honey."

She has never called him "honey" before. He hopes it's a good sign. He thinks it might be, because next she puts an arm around him and starts guiding him toward the building. They are walking so close together that they're stumbling over each other's feet, and he begins to feel happy.